APACHE RANSOM

Apache Ransom

by

Jeff Sadler

Dales Large Print Books
Long Preston, North Yorkshire,
BD23 4ND, England.

British Library Cataloguing in Publication Data.

Sadler, Jeff
    Apache ransom.

    A catalogue record of this book is
    available from the British Library

    ISBN   1-84262-119-X pbk

First published in Great Britain 2000 by Robert Hale Limited

Copyright © Jeff Sadler 2000

Cover illustration © Ballestar by arrangement with
Norma Editorial S.A.

Published in Large Print 2001 by arrangement with
Robert Hale Limited

Dales Large Print is an imprint of Library Magna Books Ltd.

Printed and bound in Great Britain by
T.J. (International) Ltd., Cornwall, PL28 8RW

ONE

Guess you could say we're like family, trouble and me. While we don't get along too well it seems like the two of us are stuck with each other, and we're never too far apart. Must be all of eight years now since I quit riding on the wrong side of the tracks and settled down to raise horses, but that old cuss won't let me be. Sooner or later I'm bound to get myself roped into some loco business or other, and trouble just naturally has to tag along.

Ramon was with me when the first of the horsemen showed. We were by the stables, looking over the little buckskin colt who'd somehow got loose from his ma and run himself up against a fencerail a few minutes back. From what we could make of it, the left forelimb had taken a bruise, but it didn't look to be anything worse.

'Nothing is broken, *señorita*,' Ramon said. He flexed the foreleg gently in those tough, calloused hands of his, like he was gripping a half-boiled egg. 'He will mend, I think.'

He glanced up, studying me closely with dark, deep-set eyes that wouldn't have been out of place on a red-tail hawk, the smile creasing up his leathery face. Ramon was a thin, rawhide-tough little stump of a feller, like some of those trees you meet out in the bad-lands, all bent and twisted from the storms and winds but still standing. He'd been wearing that same all-weather rig of scarred leather brush jacket, shotgun chaps and cartwheel-brim sombrero all the time I'd known him, and I guess it suited him just fine.

'You got it right again, Ramon,' I said. I gave him the smile back; I figured he deserved it. 'Take him away, have him tended an' rest him up a little. I'll look him over again in a while.'

'*Segura, señorita.*' Ramon eased his grip on the colt, set the hoof down carefully as the grin cut his parched-hide face. I ain't spinning no yarns when I tell you that little feller is tough as they come. Get yourself the wrong side of Ramon, you'll find he's hard as a hatchet and spikier than a Texas thicket, but around me he always has nice manners. He's the best with horses, and I reckon I ought to know. These days I can afford top wages, and I figure you get what you pay for where good hands are concerned.

That's when I looked up and saw them coming. Eight men on horseback, heading in through the gate and on towards the house. They were all of them dressed for the part, in brass-riveted Levis and faded work shirts, but they sure as hell didn't look like *vaqueros* to me.

'*Soldados, senorita?*' Ramon wanted to know. From the way the grin vanished from those rawhide features, I reckoned he'd worked out the answer.

'That's the way it looks,' I said.

I stayed watching that line of horsemen head closer. Back in the old days I broke horses for the army, and in or out of uniform that stiff poker-backed style of riding singles out a 'soldier!' from a half-mile off. That was the way I read it. And right then and there I knew it had to be trouble for me.

After a while they were close, upright shapes of the riders showing hard and clear against the lowering dusk, like they'd been cut from paper. Now I heard the clip of hooves on the dirt trail leading to the house, and saw the dust they kicked up drift like a veil over horses and men. Seemed like no time at all before they halted in front of us, drawing rein.

'I take it you'll be Miss Soledad,' the first rider said. He looked me over with the words, his glance running down from my head to my toes and all the way back again, like he was none too sure. He was tall and lean-framed, and the horse he rode made him taller still. This was a big chestnut stallion with a white blaze on the forehead, and it stamped and fretted, fighting the tight rein he was holding. The rider frowned and clenched his grip, bringing the horse's head back into line.

'You take it right, mister,' I said. Guess I might have sounded less than overjoyed. 'Kind of late for callers in this neck of the woods. What can I do for you?'

He smiled at that, and I had to allow he was worth a second glance. Under the sweat and dust his features were clean-shaven, tanned and handsome, with pale grey eyes that didn't miss a trick. His hair was grey too, cropped short and neat around the ears and the nape of the neck. I put him somewhere short of fifty, but I have to say he looked mighty good for his age.

'Colonel Harlan Thornhill, ma'am.' He ducked his head, the smile tighter as he nodded to the blond, slim young feller nearest to him. 'This is Lieutenant Sterling Armitage.'

'Glad to meet you, Miss Soledad,' the youngster touched the brim of his hat. Unlike Thornhill, he didn't smile.

'Mister Armitage.' I nodded, starting to get a mite impatient. 'If you gents will tell me what this is all about...'

'We need to talk, Miss Soledad,' Thornhill said. His pale gaze left me and touched on Ramon, waiting by the colt. 'In private, if you don't mind.'

'Anythin' you got to tell me, I reckon Ramon can hear it,' I told him. Up on the big chestnut horse Thornhill shook his head.

'I think not,' the tall feller spared Ramon the quickest of glances, and cut back to me again. 'In the meantime, if you would oblige us, we shall require food and shelter for the night. We intend to move out at first light.'

'Now just a minute, colonel!' This soldier rubbed me worse than a burr in a blanket, and it showed in my voice. 'All found for eight men an' horses don't come free, you hear? An' it don't come cheap neither!'

'No need to trouble, Miss Soledad. We'll pay whatever is necessary.' Thornhill flicked a white-gloved hand like he was getting rid of a speck of dust. He called out to one of the horsemen further back.

'Sergeant Burgin! Have the men stand down. We'll be staying the night here.'

'Sir!' Burgin whipped up his arm in salute. He was burly and thickset, with a battered rawhide face that looked like it had fought a war all by itself. He yelled at the cluster of troopers behind him. 'Troop, dismount!'

Watching those soldier boys swing down from their saddles and land stiff to attention by their horses, I wondered why they'd bothered to leave their uniforms at home. Right now, though, I was more interested in Thornhill and Armitage, who climbed down to join me, keeping a hold on the reins of their mounts. The chestnut horse still battled, trying to get loose.

'Be better if you gave him a little slack there, colonel,' I told Thornhill. 'Way you're holdin' him now, he can't hardly breathe.'

'He'll learn to obey me, Miss Soledad.' Thornhill had quit smiling for once. 'Animals need discipline just as much as we do. It's my aim to make sure they get it.'

'Have it your way.' I gave up on that skirmish for the moment, turning to Ramon. 'Take their horses, *amigo* an' show the men their quarters. Reckon we got room in the bunkhouse. These two gents are with me.'

'As you wish, *señorita*.' Ramon bowed his head, hawkish eyes watchful on the two men in front. 'If you will permit me, *señores*.'

He took the halters, leading the horses away. Like I'd figured, he gave the chestnut stallion a longer rein, the animal going along with him as quiet as you please. The buckskin colt stepped beside him, still favouring its left foreleg, and the bunch of soldiers followed. I started for the house with Thornhill and Armitage close behind. The minute we were through the door, I let them have it.

'Just what the hell is this?' I blasted off at them like a 10-gauge Greener, so steamed up I could barely wait to give them both barrels. 'You turn up here without so much as tip your hat, an' invite yourselves to bed an' board. Worse than that, you just insulted my top hand, an' that I don't care for no way. So let's hear what's so private Ramon ain't allowed to hear it?'

'We need your help, Miss Soledad,' Armitage said.

This was about the nearest to good manners I'd had from them so far, and I studied him a little closer. Armitage was your everyday shave-tail lieutenant, with wide blue eyes and a freckled boyish face razored clean of stubble, his corn-yellow hair worn long, Custer fashion, under the Stetson's brim. He wore that hat cocked slantways, and his yellow bandanna was fixed real neat with a silver stick pin. No way he'd pass for a cowhand, range rig or not. What struck me this minute was that, unlike his boss, Armitage wasn't acting tough. Matter of fact, he looked kind of worried, and seeing him that way was enough to simmer me down a shade.

'Suppose you tell me about it,' I said.

Armitage was set to speak again, but Thornhill sent him a glance you could have cut brush with, and the kid stayed quiet.

'I'll handle this, lieutenant,' the colonel said. He tugged out a chair from under the table cool as you please, setting himself down, and ran the rule over me with those chilly grey eyes. 'News travels, Miss Soledad, even to places like this. I daresay you've heard of the renegade they call Snake?'

'Serpiente, you mean?' I nodded. 'Sure, I heard of him. Apache war-leader, broke out from San Carlos a couple of months back. Last word I had, him an' his bunch was forted up in the Mogollons someplace.

Seems like the army's had trouble getting him out of there.'

'That's because he chooses to lie low and hide himself!' This time Armitage couldn't keep quiet, his face flushing hot. Seemed I'd stung him, and no mistake. 'His kind thrive on cowardly sneak attacks, hitting and running away. They won't stand and fight!'

I heard him out, saying nothing. Guess I could have told Armitage that I'd been tracking in Apache country before he cut his teeth, and I'd seen my share of stand-up fights there by the time he quit messing his diapers. Somehow, though, I doubted he'd want to hear it.

'If you don't mind, Armitage,' Thornhill's voice cut the youngster short. He leaned back in his chair, chilly eyes flexing on me again.

'As it happens, Miss Soledad, we have other concerns regarding Snake and his confederates. A week ago his band abducted a young white woman, a Miss Lydia Mansfield. She was captured while out riding alone in the mountain foothills.' He paused, his handsome features growing a sombre look. 'Miss Mansfield is my step-daughter, Miss Soledad. I raised her from a child when she was entrusted to me by her dying

15

father, an old army comrade. As you can imagine, I am most anxious for her safe return.'

'Sure, colonel. That I can understand,' I said. Inside I was trying to figure out how any female could be so dumb as to be riding in the Mogollons with wild Apaches around, but if there's one thing I've learned it's that sometimes it pays to keep your thoughts to yourself.

'Since then we've had word from Snake,' Thornhill told me. By now he was looking mighty grim. 'His band sent a message to the fort with a Navajo woman, one of a group who come in to trade. It appears he's willing to return my daughter unharmed, on one condition.'

'So what is it he wants from you?' I asked. I reckon I knew what was coming, and it didn't make it any better when he proved me right.

'He's asked for twenty horses,' the colonel told me. 'Twenty good horses, or she dies. Those were his words. You have the best horses in this part of the country, Miss Soledad.'

'Twenty horses? Did I hear you right?' Up until then I'd been feeling kind of sorry for Miss Mansfield, but now I had my own hide

16

to think of. 'Maybe they just fed you gents a bite of locoweed, but I ain't crazy yet. Twenty horses! That's gonna make a hole in my herd, ain't it?'

'Snake gives us no choice, I'm afraid.' Thornhill sounded almost regretful, but not quite. 'Difficult as the situation is, I trust you'll help us.'

'Well, now.' I didn't know what to tell him. This business had knocked my saddle sideways, and that was the truth. 'You want horses from me, colonel, you better be ready to pay for 'em. None of your army IOUs or credit notes neither!'

'How much, Miss Soledad?' Thornhill asked. I told him.

'Consider it done.' The colonel drew out a heavy billfold and unlatched it, face grim as he counted out the tens and twenties and hundreds, heaping them in a thick mound on the table top. 'I trust you'll find this satisfactory?'

I said nothing, letting the money lie.

'Miss Soledad!' Armitage's face was hotter than ever. 'I must say, ma'am, your attitude shocks me greatly. Bickering over money when a woman's life is at stake!'

'Ain't a charity, mister,' I told him. 'From what I heard, I feel mighty sorry for the lady

17

too, but this here is a business an' good horses cost money.' I nodded to Thornhill, and moved in for the *dinero* on the table. 'Looks like you got yourself a deal, colonel. I'll have 'em picked out for you myself before first light.'

I'd nearly reached the money when he shook his head, and closed his hand over the heap of notes in front of him.

'One more thing,' Thornhill said. 'You come with us when we leave. They tell me you're the best with horses, and it could be we'll need your help.'

Now I reckoned I'd heard it all, and I stared at the colonel like he'd just slugged me with a blacksmith's hammer.

'You serious?' I had trouble getting the words out. Meeting my eyes, the tall man nodded.

'I assure you I'm entirely serious, Miss Soledad. It's part of our deal.' He took a breath, that grey stare a mite impatient. 'Are you in, or out?'

'Now I know you're crazy, mister!' He'd lit the tinder and I flared up all over again. 'I got a horse ranch to run here, Thornhill! No way I aim to go chasin' round the Mogollon Rim lookin' for wild Apaches. I ain't loco yet, colonel, an' I reckon I heard enough.

Time I showed you fellers the door!'

I broke off, catching my breath and feeling my face hot up like the inside of an oven. Thornhill never made a move. Just sat there in his seat by the table, waiting for me to quit.

'I wouldn't advise it, Miss Soledad,' the colonel said. 'You and I know that nowadays most of your transactions are with the army. I'm in a position to have those contracts revoked, and I won't hestitate to do so if you give me a wrong answer now.'

'Hell, colonel! This is blackmail!'

'That's right,' Thornhill nodded, stony-faced. 'Believe me, we have plenty of other takers.'

'None as good, I'm willin' to bet.'

'Perhaps not,' the tall man allowed. 'All the same, it's something we might just overlook. Well, lady, what's it to be?'

I shook my head, still feeling kind of dazed. Any way I came at it, he held all the aces. 'Looks like you got me treed,' I told him. 'Reckon I got no choice but to take your deal, Thornhill, but don't think I come cheap. You got food an' lodgin' to pay on top of the sale, an' if I'm gonna be runnin' horses for you boys in the mountains, you'll have to pay me too.'

'This is outrageous!' Armitage spluttered, ready to explode. 'Miss Mansfield in mortal danger, and here you are holding the Army to ransom!'

'This ain't the army though, is it?' I said. Right away Thornhill smiled.

'You're an astute woman, I see.' He eased his grip on the money, drawing his hand away as a faint smile lit those handsome features. 'You're right, of course. There's no way the Army would back a transaction of this kind, paying ransom to a known renegade, but at present I'm here as a father, and my first thought is for Lydia's safety. This money is my own, and I shall count any expense worthwhile if it ensures her safe return. So name your price, Miss Soledad. I'm more than prepared to meet it.'

I thought about that young gal, alone in the Mogollons with Serpiente and his bunch, and guess I felt a little ashamed.

'Okay, Thornhill,' I told him. 'Maybe I ain't made of stone neither. I take for the twenty horses, but the rest's on the house. An' when we ride out, whatever goes for your troopers is good enough for me. Don't mean to say I have to like it, mind.'

'That was well said, Miss Soledad,' the

lieutenant murmured. Thornhill smiled and got out of his chair, handing the money over.

'That's good to hear.' He shook hands firmly, pushing the wad of bills my way. 'This was my idea in the beginning, of course, but Lieutenant Armitage offered his services, and between us we've managed to present it as a secret mission. That's all the others know about it right now.' Standing off, he frowned thoughtfully. 'The troop leaves at first light, to rendezvous with our scouts on the Verde river. Snake will send word of where the exchange is to take place, once you're into the mountains. That will be down to Armitage and yourself, of course.'

'You mean you ain't goin' with us?' I began.

'Unfortunately not.' Thornhill shook his head. 'My presence is needed at the fort. Armitage will be taking charge from now on. Right, lieutenant?'

'I shall do my best, sir.' The kid thrust out his chest, trying to look as tough as he could. Can't say he convinced me over-much, but I didn't have time to think about it as Thornhill shook my hand like he couldn't let go.

'I'd like to thank you, Miss Soledad,' the

tall feller was saying. 'Without you this mission might not have gone ahead. And it must succeed. A woman's life, my daughter's life, is in the utmost danger.'

'Reckon I know how she feels, colonel.' I stowed the money in my shirt, releasing his hand to head for the door. 'You fellers best stay put while I look out your horses. I'd best see Ramon, too, he'll be runnin' things here for a while.'

'As you wish, ma'am.' Thornhill settled back in the chair, Armitage touching a hand to his hat as I went by. But it wasn't them I was thinking about as I opened the door and stepped on through.

Trouble had come to call tonight. As I went through that door I felt him go right along with me. And I knew we'd be riding double come daylight.

TWO

'There it is, Miss Soledad! There's the Verde river!' Armitage sounded like he'd stumbled on a fortune, unable to keep the excitement out of his voice. 'We should be meeting up with our scouts any time now!'

He edged his tall roan horse out from the oak and juniper that crested the slope, and stood in his stirrups to take a look. Down below the river lay waiting just like he said, a slow snake of water winding greenish-brown and steady through the screen of cottonwoods and willows, sun dazzling off it where it hit through gaps in the trees. By now it was close to noon and that sun stood high and fierce overhead, scorching our heads and shoulders like somebody had just up-ended a bucket of boiling pitch over us both. I could have told him I'd spotted the river through the trees for a half-hour and more, but it seemed kind of mean to spoil his fun, him being so excited and all.

'Looks like you're right,' I said. 'Let's hope the rest goes as smooth.'

He didn't answer right off, still peering at the Verde. His face was hot and flushed, and those blue eyes of his were mighty pleased. Last time I'd seen a look like that was on a ten-year-old kid I caught robbing a bird's nest in the orchard at Gila Bend. I hadn't expected it on a soldier's face, here in Apache country.

'That's the spirit, Miss Soledad!' Armitage beamed giving the sun a contest. He loosened rein, letting the horse take him forward. 'Let's get down there and meet the scouts!'

I touched heels to my blackstripe dun and followed, shaking my head as I went. Way Armitage was carrying on, you'd think he'd just found America like that Columbus feller did one time. Sure, he was a decent enough sort, and he'd be even better once he got that poker out of his butt. Trouble was, I figured running horses in hostile country wasn't work for kids. Since we'd left the ranch at first light, I'd been thinking real hard about that.

Behind us Burgin and the troop headed out from the trees with my twenty horses. The herd moved ahead, close but not too tight, dust from the slope puffing and swirling over them in a cloud. Eager heads swung my way, eyes bright and ears pricked as they broke from the trees, sun gleaming on their flanks and haunches. Most were browns, with a couple of bays thrown in. All solid colours, the way the army liked it. I have to tell you those critters made a mighty pretty sight, like good horseflesh always does. I only hoped they took Snake's fancy once we met up with him. Not that I looked forward to the meeting, mind.

Burgin and the others stayed out around

them, keeping them together as they made for the Verde. The sergeant rode point with Wild, a scrawny little trooper beside him. Hood and Griffin kept watch on the flanks, and Treadwell and Calladine had the job nobody wanted, eating dust in the drag of the herd. So far they'd managed pretty fair, but they weren't *vaqueros*, and I could see things getting tougher once we were into the mountains.

'Sergeant Burgin!' Armitage called, his voice cracking above the noise of the herd. 'Have the troop move forward, we're going to the river!'

I heard Burgin's bellowing voice take up the order, and horses and escort went down the slope at a walk, Armitage and me letting them by. I wiped the sweat off my forehead with the back of my hand, holding rein on my horse as I watched them go. The black-stripe dun I rode wasn't my regular mount, but the old one had thrown a shoe the day before and was due to have a fresh one fitted. The dun was young, kind of raw and feisty, but I reckoned he'd do. I waited until Burgin and Wild were gone before easing rein, dropping in along the flank of the herd and holding my distance. That way, I figured I'd keep everything in sight. Once the horses scented water they quickened up a little, but the troopers kept them steady and they didn't run. Before you knew it, we were down to the river.

The Verde was worth a second look, sunlight bright on the water that ran smooth and easy over the stones and the floating weed. In places it showed green like its name, but it was mainly a muddy brown like most rivers I've met. Any time but this I'd have stayed a while and watched it run, with the cottonwoods and willows making their leaf-shadows on the water, but right now we had to keep those horses moving.

'Just keep 'em goin', fellers!' I called. 'Once they're far side we can let 'em drink!'

I nudged the dun forward, making for the water. From here the Verde didn't look too deep, and I figured we ought to get across. The moving bunch of horses hit the river, throwing up a spray of mud and green-white water that held rainbow colours in the sunlight. Burgin and the troopers yelled and swung their ropes, heading the group for the far bank. Peering through the spray, I caught a glimpse of two figures on the bank, and behind them a couple of ponies.

'Our scouts, Miss Soledad!' Armitage shouted.

I didn't answer, steadying the dun as it ploughed against the current. Drops of water stung my face and I sleeved my eyes clear as I rode. On the far side, one of those figures yelled and waved a hand, but the noise of the horses and their escort drowned out his voice. I saw he had a rifle cradled in the arm that didn't wave, and found myself wondering if these were our scouts, or somebody less welcome. Horse-thieves ain't exactly a rare item in Arizona, or anyplace else come to that. I had my Winchester carbine along in its saddle scabbard, and my undersized .41 Colt pistol nestled where I always carried it in the leather lining of my hip pocket. Armitage and the others were all armed up too, but for a while I felt kind of nervous. With all of us in the water, and twenty horses to look after, you might say we weren't best placed to fight off an ambush.

First of the horses were near to land, the soldiers yelling and urging them forward, when one of the browns lurched and stumbled, almost going down. Guess he must have clipped a stone, or stepped in a mud-hole he couldn't see. He staggered sideways, whinnying in fright, and hit against Wild, who was nearest. The trooper reined his mount aside and lashed with his halter-rope. It cut the brown horse hard across the nose, and the critter screamed and stumbled again, holding up the bunch behind. Wild turned his horse, coming in for another try with the long rope swinging in his hand.

'That's enough, goddamn it!' I shouted. I drove my dun towards him, my blood boiling up hotter than fire. 'Leave him be, you hear?'

Beyond me the other troopers slowed, struggling to keep the herd together as scared horses bunched and baulked in the flowing current. Wild swung round as I got close, and fixed me with a dark, mean-eyed stare.

'Just leave him, feller,' I told him. 'He's scared, is all.'

'Do as she says, trooper.' Amitage spoke tightly, reining in alongside.

Wild glared back, his long rein hefted to swing like he wasn't about to pay either of us too much mind. He was thin and small, with a long hook-nosed face and a hank of hair that dropped down into his eyes. Matter of fact, he looked more than a little like a horse himself, and it seemed kind of strange to me he should want to treat them so mean.

'Goddamn critter nearly had me down.' Wild didn't lower the rope, eyeing me and Armitage like he just might take a lick at us instead. Then the harsh voice of Burgin cut in.

'You heard the lieutenant!' the non-com snapped. 'Let the horse be, an' git this herd to land. Do it, soldier!'

I was right up with him when he turned, and got the chance to take a real good look at Sergeant Burgin close to hand. Let me tell you, it ain't a job I'd go looking to find, given choice. Burgin was huge, the biggest man in the unit by a head and more, and what there was seemed mighty scary this close to home. Muscles strained that shirt so tight it looked ready to pop its buttons, and the face above it was fierce enough to kill all by itself. His features were dark and leather-hard, pitted with old scars, and he had the coldest pair of steel-blue eyes you ever saw. If I'd been a mountain lion and come on Burgin, I reckon I'd have turned and run for my life. Reckon that's how Wild saw it, too.

That mean, defiant look went from Wild's face, and he flinched like he'd just been whipped himself. He turned in a hurry and joined the troop as they guided the horses up the bank. The brown had regained his feet and didn't look to be hurt bad. He moved on to land with the rest, water sluicing off his flanks and legs. The herd grouped at the river's edge, the troopers standing guard as Armitage and me came ashore to join them.

The pair up on the bank hadn't moved, waiting for us as we splashed to land and walked our horses forward through the sparse *galleta* and *toboso* grass to meet them. Once we got closer, I saw it was a man and woman standing there, and both of them grinning fit to bust.

'See you fellers made it,' the *hombre* said. He eased one hand clear of the long-barrelled rifle, leaving the other to cradle it across his body as the grin cracked his weathered face apart. 'You'll be the officer, right?'

'Lieutenant Sterling Armitage.' The kid stiffened up in the saddle, reddening and bristling as he answered. He sure as hell had that poker fixed in place, I thought. 'A good afternoon to you, mister...'

'Isaac Buford's the name, lieutenant.' The feller was solid and thickset, rigged in fringed buckskins that looked like they'd seen plenty of wear. He was shod with

Indian moccasins, and his face was shadowed by a broad-brimmed hat with a clutch of feathers in its band. It was that face that held me the longest. Back of the grin it was broad-featured and dark, way darker than any Indian I'd met, and the eyes glinted like crumbs of glass. 'Figure you kin call me Ike, it's a handle I answer to.' He paused, nodding to the woman who stood behind him, close to the two Indian ponies who waited ground-reined with their ropes trailing to the floor. 'This here's Conchita, folks. Reckon her an' me are the scouts you come here to find.'

Conchita didn't say a word, eyeing us carefully and smiling behind her hand. She was all Indian from the look of her, small and slender and hawkish-faced in a worn buckskin shift and fringed leggings, the black hair tied back in a gleaming horsetail. Armitage said nothing either, looking her over like he didn't believe what he saw. Whatever Thornhill had told him to expect, I could tell this wasn't it.

'Just read your mind there, lieutenant,' Buford shook back the thick, greying hair that fell in a single heavy plait over one shoulder. He still hadn't lost that lazy grin. 'Fact is, you'd be wrong. Conchita is a

Lipan Apache, she knows the language and the country better'n anybody else you're gonna meet out here. She kin ride an' shoot good, an' the two of us are kind of close.' He glanced back towards her, nodded as she sent him an answering smile. 'Take one of us, lieutenant, you take both. Get my drift?'

'I believe I understand you, Mr Buford.' Armitage cut out the words stiffer than he sat his horse; guess that poker was paining him worse than any of us knew. 'This is Miss Soledad, she's come to help with the herd.'

'Pleased to meet you, Mr Buford,' I said.

'Ma'am,' Buford touched the brim of his hat, the grin slowly edging away as he eyed me real close. Guess it wasn't too often he got to see a woman rigged out in a man's work shirt and cord pants, riding along with a bunch of soldiers. 'Horse dealer, huh?'

'That's right.' I met his look head-on, scanning those dark, weatherbeaten features. By now I reckoned I had the answer. Buford was one of those Seminole scouts the army had used down on the Texas border after the war ended between the states. Word had it they were mostly a mixture of Indian and runaway slaves who'd been brought up as Seminoles themselves, and as scouts they had quite a reputation. Up to now I'd never set eyes on one, but I was ready to bet money that Buford fitted the pattern. And from the way he eyed me, he hadn't learned that slave trick of looking away.

'If it's all the same to you, Mr Buford, I'll stand down the troop.' Armitage was getting to sound kind of impatient. 'Sergeant Burgin, have the men stand down and water the horses. We'll be staying here for the next couple of hours! Once the troop is rested, we'll move on.'

'Yessir!' Burgin saluted, his face tight and hard as a brass-bound chest. The veteran bellowed at the bunch of troopers behind him. 'Troop, dismount! Off saddles, an' water the horses! We're makin' camp!'

He swung down from the horse, his massive figure looming above the rest of the troop as he led them for the river. In front of Armitage and me, Isaac Buford still hadn't moved, but now the grin had vanished.

'Best we don't stick around here too long, lieutenant.' The scout frowned, dark eyes shifting warily to Armitage again. 'Snake's right at home in this country, an' he knows just where to hide. Should he catch us here with our backs to the Verde, we ain't gonna have a prayer.'

Half-way to the river, I saw Burgin halt and turn around. Watching him, I remembered why I'd been glad he'd just turned his back. That soldier raised the hair on my neck worse than any feller I've seen in my life.

'Permission to speak, lieutenant!' Burgin called. While he made it sound respectful, his voice had a lash that made sure he had our attention. 'We've come a ways to get here, sir. Men an' horses are both of 'em worn out. I reckon we could use the rest.'

'Thank you, sergeant. That will be all.' Armitage answered him tight-lipped, his slim frame ramrod-stiff in the saddle. I got the feeling he wasn't finding it any easier than me to meet those steely eyes. Burgin saluted and turned back for the river, and Armitage eased out a breath, his own blue-eyed stare coming back to Buford again.

'I see no prospect of an Indian attack, Mr Buford,' the shave-tail said. His glance raked the scout over like he'd just crawled out from under a stone someplace. 'We already have a deal with Snake, and it seems to me he's unlikely to break the agreement.'

'You reckon?' Buford considered the kid in the saddle above him, his head to one side.

'Maybe he's gonna keep the woman an' take the horses anyhow. You thought about that, lieutenant?'

Armitage sucked in his breath like he'd just been slapped, and for a minute he looked ready to dive from his horse and start a fight he'd be bound to lose. Then the blond kid hauled back, teeth set tight as he breathed out again.

'They tell you how he got that name of his, Armitage?' Buford asked. 'You know how come they call him Snake?'

Armitage said nothing, still simmering like a well-fired skillet. From the look on his face I could tell he hadn't heard.

'Sure, I know,' I slipped feet from the stirrups, swinging myself down as I answered. 'Serpiente got it from the Mex ranchers he raided across the border. They call him Snake on account of he's quiet an' kills real quick, an' you never know just where he's laired up until you tread on him, an' he bites. Do I have that right?' I caught the sideways look he gave me, and fought back a smile.

'Yeah,' Buford eyed me thoughtfully 'See you been around, lady. An' as it happens, you're dead right.' He switched his gaze to Armitage, who still sat his mount, smouldering. 'That's just the way Snake is, lieutenant. An' right now he's out yonder, waitin'.'

'You mean you found tracks?' the kid demanded. Buford grinned, shaking his grizzled head.

'Not so's you'd notice.' He kept to the grin, studying the shave-tail like he was up against some cocky kid in short pants. Buford glanced away through the stands of timber to those thick forested slopes that climbed up for the peaks of the Mogollons, as if he aimed to catch sight of whatever lay hidden there. He shifted the look back to Armitage, the brief grin fading. 'Only thing is, I got a real itchy feelin' like a blowfly just lit on the back of my neck.'

'A feeling, you say?' Armitage couldn't keep the contempt out of his voice. If he'd set out to make an enemy of Buford from the first, he couldn't have handled it better, and from the scowl on his stubbled features that was how Buford saw it too.

'Sure, that's right. A feelin'.' The scout sounded like he was running out of patience. 'Once you been long in this line of work, you learn to trust it. Best keep our eyes peeled from here on in!'

He glared up at the blond kid, fierce as a

wolverine, but Armitage didn't turn a hair, his answer coming out just as clipped and stiff as always.

'I'll bear that in mind, Buford,' Armitage told him. Sound of his voice made it plain he wasn't about to give it too much thought. 'In the meantime, if you'll excuse me, I think it's time I dismounted and joined the rest of my troop.'

He kicked from the stirrup and swung down from his fretting mount, keeping a hold on the halter-rope as he went. Buford cut him a look that would have left a Gila monster stone-dead and turned from us, gathering the rifle in both his hands. Weapon was an old pattern Henry, kind of worn and battered at first sight, but I guessed that come the time it would work all right.

'Just who in hell is the goddamn scout around here?' the Seminole muttered. He signed to Conchita, and the two of them took up the ropes of their ponies, leading the animals away from us towards the trees. Armitage watched them go, his boyish face still hot.

'Damned impertinence!' The lieutenant sounded sore. He didn't look at me, his eyes following the vanishing backs of the scouts and their horses. 'Fellow's barely more than a savage himself. Doesn't he realize this mission has been thoroughly planned beforehand?'

'Reckon he sees it different, is all,' I said.

I didn't bother telling him Buford wasn't on his own. To be honest, I was beginning to see things pretty much the same way myself. Planning on this trip was half-assed at best, especially as we were counting on Snake to set up the meeting-place. If there was one thing Snake wasn't, it was dumb. Trouble was, I could be none too sure the same was true of Armitage. But I figured this minute wasn't the best of times to mention it.

Hood and Griffin sloped on past, leading their tired mounts to the river. Wasn't the first time I'd noticed how the pair of them hung together, while the others formed a separate bunch of their own, but I guessed I'd still to find out why. At first glance you couldn't have hit on a more ill-assorted pair. Griffin was skinny and balding, looking forty at least, while Hood was a smooth-featured kid whose folks wouldn't have let him out the house a couple of years back. But then there ain't no accounting for taste in the army, or anyplace else.

Beyond them the other troopers of the

unit stooped and drank from the waters of the Verde, their horses and mine standing with heads lowered as they quenched their thirst. I reckoned I'd been stood around here long enough, with the blackstripe dun fretting at the end of its rope. No sense in waiting until the herd drank itself water-logged, or Snake might find himself a few horses short. I turned around and followed Hood and Griffin, the dun horse stepping after me towards the river.

Burgin got there before us, halting to ease rein on his mount as it dipped its muzzle into the water. Calladine and Treadwell were on hands and knees at the river's edge, drinking. A short distance from them the horse-faced Wild cupped his hands to bring the water to his mouth. Burgin stood hands on hips and scanned the line of trees far side of the river.

'Hey, Burgin!' Calladine glanced up from where he knelt by the sergeant's feet, filling his hat with water that he splashed on his stubbled, dust-coated face. 'How long before we change places ridin' with this goddamn herd? Treadwell an' me been eatin' dust for the best part of the day now!'

He stared up at Burgin, wiping his wet face with a grimy sleeve. Calladine was a burly feller, running to fat at the waist, with a ruddy face and cropped ash-blond hair that looked like a stubble-cut field. Eyes that peered out of the dust and the smears of water were pale and hard as pebbles. Anybody but Burgin might have been worried by them, but I reckon Burgin wasn't anybody.

'That's right enough,' Treadwell dabbed at his face with a soaked neckerchief, scowling through the grime. He was a tall, lanky redhead with strange coloured eyes, kind of yellowish-brown, that looked you all the way through. 'Time somebody else rode drag, ain't it?'

Burgin gave them one of his mean stares, and the pair of them went mighty quiet.

'You boys listen to me real close,' Burgin said. 'Far as you're concerned, I got one name, an' it's sergeant. When it comes to ridin' drag, or anythin' else, you fellers do like I tell you or by God you're gonna regret it.' He paused, that cold gaze shifting from one to the other, like he was waiting. 'Now, you both hear me good?'

'Sure, sergeant,' Calladine scowled, looking away. Far side of him Treadwell nodded, those yellow-brown eyes wary on the non-com.

'That's better.' Burgin glanced to Wild, who knelt watching him with both cupped hands lifted. 'Goes for you too, Wild.'

'I hear you, sergeant,' Wild still looked scared. Burgin appeared not to notice, crouching down by his horse to trail a hand in the water and bring it to his lips. I took a few paces from them, standing to peer into the flowing river as my horse bent its head to drink. What looked back up at me wasn't too much of a surprise. Female I saw there was tall and dark complexioned just like me, rigged in the same shirt and cords, with a smooth, high-boned face and slender frame with curves enough to pass muster with most fellers I've met. Hair under the Stetson was long and straight, with a blue-black sheen, and her dark eyes stared up into mine. Reckon she looked just as puzzled as I did, too.

Soledad, I told her, you sure as hell messed up this time around. Always figured you for a smart one, girl. How come you had to end up here?

I spoke to her quietly in my mind, so none of the others heard, but her face didn't change. She stared back up at me as troubled as before, and I knew that neither her nor the river could give me any answers.

THREE

'Yeah. He's been here, right enough,' Ike Buford said.

He glanced up from where he crouched on the ground, holding the pinto pony by its long halter-rope as his eyes came back to meet us. Buford nodded to the snapped-off sapling in front of him, its bark peeled off to show the white of the inner wood.

'No way that sapling got itself bust by accident, lieutenant. The son of a bitch is puttin' down markers for us, I reckon.'

Armitage sat his horse a while in silence, his slim frame ramrod-straight and not moving a muscle as he listened. I held rein on my blackstripe dun beside him, Conchita silent on my right while Burgin and the troop held the horse herd penned behind. Wasn't any too easy for them, neither. That bunch of critters were starting to fret and twitch around some, tired of standing quiet and eager to be going, and it looked to me like those soldier boys had their hands full keeping them in one place. Wasn't just they were impatient either, from what I could make of it. Maybe it had something to do with the heat. Right now it felt mighty close and sticky, the air around us humming black and thick with flies that hovered in clouds round our faces. I used a sleeve to brush the sweat out of my eyes, flipped my rope at a blue-bellied fly that came in too close for comfort. Since we left the Verde behind I figured we'd made fair progress, coming clear of the willows and the lush water meadows with their *grama* grass clusters to start on the uphill grade through stands of alder and pine, dotted with thickets of thorny brush in the spaces between. And now it looked like our scouts had picked up on the first sign of the Apaches.

'I see.' Armitage didn't sound like the news bowled him over exactly, that school-boy face wearing a look that might have made a boulder seem friendly. The kid shifted a little in his saddle, studying the trees and bushes that furred the slopes up ahead, like they didn't impress him too much either. 'And precisely what is he trying to tell us, do you think?'

'He wants us to come to him, Armitage.' The Seminole eyed the lieutenant in a tired kind of way, like it was getting to be a chore for him to explain. Buford jerked a thumb beyond the busted, pointing sapling, to where a line of pebbles caught the sunlight, glinting like steel against the sparse grass and dirt, one behind the other. 'Like I say, these here are markers – signposts, you might call 'em. Gonna find more of 'em out ahead, unless I'm mistook. Follow this trail, we'll meet up with Snake before too long.'

'That much I can understand, Mister Buford.' Armitage's voice had the chill to match a blue norther in its prime. The shave-tail glanced back to the fretful, sweating bunch of men and horses behind him, his gloved hands tight on the reins. 'Very well. You've impressed us with your knowledge, no doubt of it. Is there anything else we need to know, do you think?'

For a while the Seminole didn't say a word, his head thrown back as he sniffed at the air like a hound. He cut a glance towards Conchita, who sat her pony eyeing the sky overhead, and then turned slowly back to Armitage.

'One thing, lieutenant,' the thickset feller told him. 'Best we should get these horses to the higher ground right now. Way I read it, we're due for a storm mighty soon.' He paused, shifting his black-eyed stare to the

44

bunch of soldiers further back. 'Was I you, boys, I'd slicker up, an' fast. Reckon it's gonna be kind of wet before too long.'

Armitage frowned at that, scanning the sky where it showed through the crowns of the trees, and I guess I gave it some attention myself. At first sight it was pretty much the same as always, a deep blue overset by patches of white, floating cloud. Once I'd studied closer, I figured maybe a few extra clouds had put in an appearance, and that sky was taking on a brassy, polished look. That, and the way my twenty horses were acting up, was enough to tell me that Buford had it right. Any time a horse of mine gets restless, I start looking for trouble. But fellers like Armitage always have to work these things out for themselves, and that kind of effort appears to take one hell of a while.

'I see no sign of it, Mister Buford,' the shave-tail decided. Armitage shrugged, easing the rein on his tall roan stallion. 'Still, I daresay we had better be moving in any case.' He started the horse forward, nodding to the man who still hunkered on the ground. 'Mount up, man. You'd better show us the next set of these markers of yours, if you're sure that's what they are.'

Ike Buford got up from where he crouched by the line of stones, pushing himself slowly to his feet. The scout didn't speak, but from the way he was looking at Armitage I reckon he was thinking plenty, and none of it fit for mixed company. Away to the right a thorn bush shivered suddenly and Sergeant Burgin tensed, his hand whipping down to grip the butt of his holstered pistol. The bird swooped out of sight beyond the trees and the big non-com scowled, shifting his hand from the gun. Far side of me, Conchita flashed a smile of her own.

'Ain't nothin' but a wren, soldier.' Buford had found his old, familiar grin. The scout mounted up, cradling the long-barrelled Henry rifle in the crook of his arm as he tapped moccasined heels to the thin flanks of his pony. 'Best save on the bullets, feller, could be we'll be needin' 'em later.'

Burgin stayed dumb, that tough-looking face of his about as appetizing as a granite cliff as he measured the Seminole with his pale, chilly eyes. The big sergeant turned on the rest of the troopers, his voice bellowing out against the quiet.

'You heard the lieutenant!' Burgin yelled. 'Forward, troop, on the double! Let's git them horses movin'!'

He jabbed spurs to his horse's sides and the critter jerked forward like it had just been stung by a hornet, loping out across the meadow. Armitage, the scouts and me moved aside as the troop came through with the horse herd at a steady lick, crossing open ground between the trees. Buford and Conchita moved out ahead of them, while I stuck with the shave-tail at the flank of the herd. All twenty of my browns and bays looked to be still in pretty good shape, and that's how I aimed for them to stay. No sense taking half-dead horses to bargain with the Apache, or anybody else, come to that.

Wasn't too long before we were out from the thickets, and heading uphill through the rocks and timber stands. Every so often along the way Conchita and Buford would rein in, picking up on fresh signs that Snake and his bunch had left behind. Maybe a busted twig here, a faint scratch on a rock, or a half-smothered print of a moccasin in the dirt, all of them pointing the way ahead. Didn't take too much thought to work out that Buford had been right about them. I've tracked Apache often enough to know they don't leave that kind of sign unless they aim to be followed home.

A half-hour or so later the herd was running through a narrow gully with broken, rocky slopes rising high to either side. My blackstripe dun clipped a loose rock in the bed of the trail and all but stumbled, and I got a hold on the rein to keep him steady. Seemed to me the air had grown mighty still and heavy, pressing so tight it was tough to get a breath, and the flies were swarming worse than ever. The way they hung around us in a dark, humming cloud, I reckoned we couldn't have drawn more of them if we'd dragged a red-raw beef carcass along behind. I swatted a cluster of them off my face, spitting out a couple that aimed to get even closer. You can take it from me them critters didn't taste no better than they looked.

A hot wind came fanning down the arroyo like somebody had just left open the door to a pot-bellied stove, and I felt a fresh runnel of sweat slide down into my eyes. I shook my head, blinking to see straight, and glanced up overhead. Up above the mountains a ripe bunch of thunderheads was coming our way, and that sky was getting darker every minute. Away in the distance, I caught the bright dazzle of lightning, and an answering boom of thunder, and knew we were in trouble.

'She's gonna break!' I shouted over the noise of the hooves. I touched heels to the dun's sides, heading at a run along the flank of the herd as I yelled out to the nearest of the troopers. 'Turn 'em, goddammit! Get 'em headed upslope, you hear? We got to make it to the higher ground!'

Out in front I could see the narrow mouth of the gully cutting a thin black notch between sheer walls of rock. From here it didn't look to be much more than a rifle-slit, and I reckoned we'd be lucky to run the horses through two abreast. One look at that gully mouth told me there was no way we were going to make it through to the other side. Our one chance was to drive up the slopes, and hope to hell we were in time.

Armitage heard my yelling, and reined in his mount, turning to glare back at me over his shoulder. First off he frowned like he wasn't sure he heard me right, then that kid's face of his started to set like he was ready to argue about it. By now Burgin and the troop were all staring my way, the herd slowing in a shroud of hanging dust as the point riders slewed to a halt. I stabbed a finger towards the rocky slope to our right, shouting at the full pitch of my lungs.

'Head for the high ground!' I yelled so hard I felt my throat would bust clean open. I pushed myself to the front of the column, edging in close to turn the leading horses for the slope. 'Damn it, Armitage, do it! We ain't got no time!'

I saw his face alter in a moment, and he called out to the men behind, Burgin taking up the order in his louder bellowing voice. Wild and Burgin followed my lead, shoving the horses sideways and uphill into the rocks and brush, the wide and drag riders nudging the rest of them after. Before you could take a breath the whole bunch of us were scrambling and sliding up for the rim of the slope as fast as four hooves allowed.

Way it worked out, we were none too soon. Almost as the horse herd turned uphill with the ten of us yelling and driving them on those thunderheads came piling over the mountains, and the sky turned black and ugly as a half-healed bruise. Urging the blackstripe dun up for the crest, I watched huge cloud-shadows sweep the ground, turning the world dark like someone had just put out a lamp, and guessed what was coming next. From high overhead the first heavy drops came down, spattering like fallen stars on the parched dirt all around, then the lightning hit, and the whole sky broke apart.

First strike came as a hellish burst of light that turned the gully to blue and white fire and threatened to leave me stone-blind just from seeing it. I didn't even catch sight of it forking to earth, just shut my eyes to that sudden glare and held tight to my dun horse as he bucked and squealed in fright. The thunderclap that followed sounded like I was in the bottom of a giant barrel and some son of a bitch had fired off an artillery barrage inside it. For a while I wondered if I'd ever hear again, then the echoes went blasting and whiplashing away over the mountains and I figured maybe I would. Now the rain came down, all right, a solid rush of water like they'd just emptied out all the bath-tubs in God's creation. I felt it pound my head and shoulders hard as sackfuls of sand, and pretty soon it was tough trying to see at all. That rain came hammering down in a thick grey wall, bouncing and spraying up from the ground with a drumming noise that drowned the shouts around me. In less time than it takes to spit, me and that blackstripe dun were drenched through to the bone, ploughing blind into a heavy curtain of rain as the storm broke over the gully.

Lightning bit blue-white through the downpour, set the world ablaze for the span of a heartbeat. It forked into the ground bare yards ahead, and my horse went crazy, fighting the rein. I swore, wrestling him into line as the thunder slammed and racketed to set my ears ringing again. In front I could make out the moving shapes of men and horses, shadows in the pounding fall of rain. Once the thunder quit, you couldn't hear for the hiss and drumming of the downpour all around. Under me the dun hit loose rocks and slithered to stand, and I had trouble getting him moving again. Next dazzle of lightning showed me the first trickles of run-off sliding down from the crest to meet us, bringing their stones and dirt along and turning the ground to a mantrap. Pretty soon they were swelling into streams of their own. Below, down in the bed of the gully, came a deeper, swelling rumble of sound as floodwater came rushing down the canyons looking for a way through.

Scatters of timber loomed out of the murk, tree-boles and branches coming at us sudden through the wall of rain. Up ahead lightning sizzled and struck in a jagged blue fork, showing me the outlines of the troop and the herd that still scrambled for the rim above. Gunblast of the thunder that came after was the loudest yet, busting out from low over my head. Second strike wasn't much more than a long-drawn breath behind it, and for a minute I thought I'd been hit. That blinding flash drove into one of the trees to my left, and I heard the deafening crack of the timber as it hit all the way down. The tree split wide open in front of my eyes, flames and smoke spouting out of the branches as it toppled over, its insides showing charred and splintered. The dun horse screamed and bucked like hell, and I fought with the wet, slippery reins to keep him steady. I might just have made it, if it hadn't been for that goddamned tree.

The black, smoking branch came at me so fast I didn't have the time to duck or holler. I felt the jolt as it clipped my shoulder on its way to earth, pitching me half out my saddle. I lost a stirrup and tried to haul back astride, but the dun bucked again and that rain-slick halter tore out of my hand. Before I could muster the breath for a decent cuss-word I was down the flank of my horse and hitting muddy dirt, rolling over and over as my own weight and the slope took me down, heading for the gully.

Now I heard the flood, blasting through the canyons with a roar loud enough to shake the ears loose from my head. Rolling, I saw it rip through that gully at the height of a man on horseback and travelling twice as fast, a filthy mud-coloured tide of water that pitched boulders and pine trunks and deer carcasses along without stopping to take a breath. I don't mind telling you it scared the hell out of me. I yelled and clawed as I went ploughing down to meet it, grabbing at rocks and tree boughs that slipped or tugged out of my hands, but I knew I hadn't a hope. The whole of the slope was churned like oatmeal porridge from the pounding of the rain, and a fair hunk of it slid right along with me into the flood that went shooting past underneath. I was still snatching out, helpless and trying for a hold that wasn't there, when I shot down into the water like a 'gator on a mud-slide, and that flood was towing me along so fast that it was a fight to stay breathing.

That wave hit me hard as a blacksmith's sledge, hammered me flat to send me underwater. It was like I didn't weigh no more than a feather in the wind. The current picked me up and carried me along, throwing me against a boulder clump that lay close to the water's edge. I'd just floundered up to the surface, spluttering out a peck of muddy water, when it dumped me there and slapped the breath out of me. Just for a split second I was wedged into a gap between those rocks, and that's all that saved me, I reckon. Anything but that, and I'd have been a goner. As it was, I latched on to the biggest rock I could get my arms around, and hugged the goddamn thing so tight you might think the pair of us were spoken for.

Noise of the flash flood went booming through the gully, matched by the racket of thunder and the bright flares of lightning overhead. I shook the water from my eyes and saw the rush of that wave go by and around me, rolling logs and tree limbs and whatever else had the bad luck to get in its way. It did its damnedest to suck me clear off that rock and carry me along with the rest, but the boulder clump held firm, and I guess I stuck with it.

Carcass of some poor critter floated by me belly-up with its legs in the air – white-tail deer, from what I could make of it – and the sight turned me kind of sick. Noise of the flash flood drowned out the rain, and even the thunder sounded like it was some distance off, but I can't say that it troubled me overmuch at the time. I watched that tide of water and the heap of trash it carried tear on towards the gully mouth, blasting through that narrow gap with the wave backed up to the height of a house and spray and hunks of tree and rock flying up the walls on either side. Fixed as I was, I still had to be thankful it hadn't caught up with me there. Pushed into a gap that tight, the water would have hit like a bullet, and I reckon I wouldn't have had a prayer.

Away through that pelting curtain of rain, some-place higher up the slope, I caught sight of something moving. Kind of a grey shadow-shape at first, but pretty soon it got closer and I made out the figure of a man on horseback. Peering through the downpour I saw the scout, Ike Buford, with Conchita following right behind him. Same time I glimpsed them he got down from his pony and began unslinging a couple of lariats from the saddlehorn. I clung to that rock tighter than the Reaper hugs a dying man, watching as the Seminole tied one lariat around his middle, playing out the rope to Conchita, who made the far end fast around one of the trees on the crest. Buford took hold of the second lariat and started down towards me, swinging the rope into a loop above his head as his moccasined feet slithered in the mud. As far as I could tell he was trying to call out to me as he came, but I knew there wasn't a hope in hell of me hearing whatever it was he had to say.

Don't you worry none, feller, I thought to myself. Ain't no way I aim to let go of this rock. Not if I can help it, anyhow.

That current still grabbed and hauled at me, fighting to pull me away from the rock. I could feel the wet stone start to slip under my fingers, and dug into it with my nails as all my muscles clenched up tight. Buford built a loop and planted his heels in the mud, leaning forward to throw. First try missed and struck the water and he dragged it back in a hurry. Ike Buford stood straight again, whirling the lariat round his head in the hammering rain, water spraying up from the rope as it spun. I took a quick look backwards over my shoulder and almost died right there and then.

A bunch of snakes came floating past, swept along by the force of the wave, close enough for me to see those pretty diamond markings they had. Every one of those critters was a diamondback rattler, and I figured they were none of them in a friendly frame of mind. Flash flood must have washed their nest away, and now they were swimming along towards me. I hollered into the rain for Ike to make it fast, knowing all the time he couldn't hear a word, and got ready for the worst.

One of those rattlers came within an arm's reach of me, and that's plenty close enough, better believe it. He reared up as he floated by and opened his mouth, showing me a mighty fine set of fangs. They were something to admire, all right, but I sure as hell wasn't in no mood to see them. Rattler was aiming for a strike when the current caught up with him and sent him scudding after his pals, heading for the gully mouth. I swear the breath I loosed off afterwards drowned even the thunder and the noise of the flood. For a while I couldn't see a thing, but whether it was sweat or water I can't rightly tell. Best you folks should work that one out for yourselves, I reckon. Take it from me, I was mighty glad to see them critters go by.

Height of the water dipped lower around me as the flood-wave spent itself, and it seemed like the thunder died down a shade, racketing further off above the mountains.

Worst of the rain had begun to slacken off as Buford tried again, and this time he got it right. The rawhide rope dropped down past my shoulders and I wriggled my body to keep both arms free as it fell lower, drawing tight across my chest. Buford leaned back and hauled and I said a prayer as my hands slipped off the rock. Force of the water grabbed me and towed me quite a distance, but Ike was pretty well anchored to that tree on the crest, and now Conchita got a grip on the rope to pull along with him. They hauled me back against the last of the current, dragging me through the shallows and on to land. I felt the last fierce jerk as my body left the water and hit thick, rain-sodden mud. I landed face-down my whole length, and I tell you feller there ain't no time mud's tasted so sweet to me in all of my life.

Buford and Conchita dragged me clear of the water and higher up the slope, then loosed off the rope and let me lie. I stayed there for a while, coughing and spewing all manner of stuff I don't hardly care to mention, with my hair plastered down into my eyes, my hat hanging halfway round my neck on its cord, and enough water in my shirt and denim pants to sink a riverboat. It was a couple of minutes at least before I found the strength to lift my head, and when I did Conchita and the Seminole were still standing there looking down at me. Behind them I made out the figure of Armitage, peering over Buford's shoulder. Maybe I had it wrong, but it seemed to me the kid was looking a mite paler than he'd been before the storm broke. But then again, I guess the way I looked this minute wasn't nothing to write home about.

'Reckon you can have your rope back now,' I told Buford. I spat out the last of the mud, and wiped my mouth with the back of my hand. 'Thanks a lot, Ike. Looks like I owe you one.'

Buford's dark, broad face didn't change expression. He eyed me for a while, studying me with that black, piercing stare of his as he loosened off the lariat that cinched tight around my chest.

'You were surely lucky there, Miss Soledad,' was all he said.

'And I know it.' I staggered up on to my feet, hearing the wash of water that poured off me to the ground. First off it seemed my legs didn't want to hold me, and I sat down again in the mud, dragging off my boots and up-ending them to sluice out the water that filled them. Overhead the storm was breaking up, the thunder down to a faraway muttering as lightning stabbed faintly into the distance. The fall of rain shrank and thinned out, dwindling to a spatter of heavy drops in the mud. After a while it quit altogether and the sky cleared, dark clouds shredding away as the sun broke through. Before long my shirt and pants warmed up and steamed in the heat.

'Thanks again, Ike,' I told the scout. I hauled on my boots and struggled up and found that this time I could stand. Reaching out, I shook his hand, and Buford gave me a grin right back. Behind him, though, Armitage was still looking a little worried.

'Are you sure you are all right, Miss Soledad?' the shave-tail wanted to know. I nodded, feeling a twinge of pain in my ribs from where the wave had pitched me into the rocks. I figured I'd be carrying my share of bruises come morning, but I knew it could have been a whole lot worse.

'Sure, Armitage. I'll live,' I told him.

By now Buford had disentangled himself from the lariat around his waist, and the four of us headed back through the mud, away from the water in the gully bed. Flash flood was long gone, only a shallow brown stream choked with tree and rock litter left behind. I figured it wasn't about to last too long, not with the sun as fierce as it was. As we battled uphill through the slowly drying mud I glanced to the crest of the ridge up ahead. My horses were huddled together near a stand of sycamores, and Burgin and the five troopers sat their own mounts, waiting like a bunch of rainsoaked crows. Their sodden clothes and the hides of the horses sent up a mighty cloud of steam in the sunshine. I started counting the horses as I walked towards them, and wasn't too sure whether I had it right.

'Did they get clear?' I asked. 'All of them?'

'Sure did, lady.' Ike Buford nodded, the grin cracking wider as he coiled the rope in his hands. 'Every last one. There's a few of 'em far side the rise you cain't see, is all.'

'And my dun horse? Is he okay?' I remembered the lightning, the bucking, squealing panic.

'Yeah, him too. And our ponies.' Buford's broad, leathery face gullied into laughter lines, his dark eyes twinkling. 'You're the only one we almost lost, Miss Soledad, and now it looks like we got you too, don't it?'

'You sure did,' I told him. 'Don't worry, Ike. I ain't about to forget it.'

We didn't say anything for a while, the four of us marching ahead in silence. When it broke at last, it was down to Armitage.

'Your surmise appears to have been correct, Mister Buford.' The lieutenant spat out the words like they didn't taste too good. Armitage didn't look sideways to the scout, his blue-eyed gaze fixed on the ground ahead as we slogged up for the crest. 'Thanks to Miss Soledad and yourself, it seems we have narrowly avoided a possible catastrophe. You may be sure we are all grateful to you.'

'That goes for Miss Soledad, too,' I said.

'Mighty handsome of you, Armitage.' Buford had tamed his grin just a little, but I still had the feeling he was enjoying this more than the soldier walking beside him. 'Just doin' my job, is all. Thanks all the same.'

I heard the last of the thunder rumble away beyond the Mogollon Rim, and started to feel a whole lot better. The storm and the flash flood had passed us by, and hadn't taken one of us with them. Thanks to Ike and Conchita I was out from the water with my hide. A little slapped around, maybe. My shoulder still ached from the clip that branch had given me, and there'd be one hell of a bruise on my ribs from those rocks. Kind of shaky, too, right now, but me and my clothes were drying out fast, and with any luck I might even get that pocket pistol of mine back to working in a while. Best of all, we'd come out of it with the herd still in one piece. All my twenty horses were alive and kicking, not a critter lost. That had to be good news, I thought, especially if we were due to meet up with Snake before long.

The escort sat their mounts, steaming in quiet as they watched us climb the slope towards them. Once we reached the crest they still looked like they didn't have too much to say. Burgin eyed me without a word as I went by, his craggy face not giving away what he thought. Hood and Griffin gave me a smile apiece, but the rest of the troop seemed none too pleased to see me. The way Calladine looked at me, for one, you'd think I'd called that storm up all by myself, just to make sure everybody took a dousing.

'You got lucky this time, lady,' the blond trooper said. It was pretty much what Ike Buford had told me a few minutes back, but the way Calladine made it come out it sure didn't sound the same. I looked him in the eye and didn't answer, moving on to where my blackstripe dun stood waiting in his own rising blanket of steam, but I felt a grey pebbly stare come after me as I went. I didn't miss what the blond feller muttered to his pal Treadwell either, once my back was turned.

'Horsewoman, huh?' Calladine's voice carried to me, hard-edged as lava rock. 'Cain't even stay aboard her own critter, from what I seen. What kinda help is she gonna be, you reckon?'

I heard the low-voiced chuckle of the redheaded trooper, and that temper of mine threatened to flare up any minute. I tell you, mister, it was mighty tempting for me to turn on Calladine and the rest and ask them how good they'd look if a busted branch caught them across the shoulder in a storm, but I knew I'd be wasting my time. I shut my mouth tight and kept on walking, and let the dumb sons of bitches think what the hell they liked. I was still breathing, and that was what counted for me. I hadn't come out here for any stubble-faced trooper to take a shine to me, and if Calladine and his pals hated me like poison what did it matter? Long as the deal was done with Snake and we made it back home again, why in hell should I care?

Once we'd all got our breath back Armitage kept us on the move, finding our way to the higher slopes. Buford and Conchita cast around for a while, looking for sign, but when they came back the thickset feller frowned and shook his head.

'Not a thing, lieutenant,' Buford said. The Seminole scanned the timbered ridges all around, still scowling. 'Whatever sign he left, that storm washed it out, but good. Best we make camp, an' see if he puts down fresh marks tomorrow. Nothin' much else we kin do, I guess.'

'Let's hope that he obliges us, Mister Buford.' Armitage's voice was enough to show just how put out he felt. The lieutenant fretted impatiently, slapping his rein on the back of his glove as he spoke. 'Obviously he wishes to make contact with us, from the markers we have seen.' He paused, fixing the scout with an unforgiving look. 'If no further sign is found, Mr Buford, I shall hold you responsible. As the scout for this mission...'

'Reckon I know my job, Armitage,' Ike Buford told him.

He turned his pinto pony with a touch of the rein, and rode back along the ridge, cradling his long Henry rifle. He didn't bother to look around as he went.

Nightfall found us camped on a flat grass meadow above the ridges that had a clean stream and a few stands of pines. I made sure my horses were fed and watered like they should be, and the rest of us looked after ourselves. By now we were all of us dried out from the soaking we'd had, and you wouldn't have known there'd been a storm at all. Now and then you'd hear thunder someplace further into the mountains, and a faint shiver of lightning would pale the sky, but that was some other folks' grief, I figured. I lay in my bed-roll with my head pillowed on that old Texas saddle of mine, and watched the moon ride up over the Mogollon Rim like a prime silver dollar in the sky. Just being alive felt mighty good to me, and when I closed my eyes I reckon I was still smiling. I slept the night through like a baby, and all the while I was dreaming of running horses.

Next morning when I opened my eyes, I recalled that storm a whole lot better than the night before. Bruises on my ribs and shoulder had come out in spades, and my head was thudding like the inside of a bandsman's drum. I figured I wasn't about to win no Miss Fourth of July contest this morning neither, and when I struggled out from my bed-roll it hurt me just to breathe. Once I got up on my feet, it didn't feel much better.

Could be worse, girl, I told myself. At least you're still breathing, and them bruises are going to fade in a while.

Away into the trees a blue jay screamed, and my head rang like a belltower with the sound. I shielded my eyes against the sun, and looked around me. What I saw was the Mogollons making a knife-edge on the sky, and a whole lot of ridges and timber every which way I turned around. Somewhere out there friend Snake was waiting with Miss Mansfield for his twenty horses. I touched the sore place on my ribs and flinched, remembering how close I'd come to not being here at all.

Let's hope it don't get no worse, I thought.

Into the woods, I heard that damned jay scream again.

FOUR

Most times, trouble starts off kind of small. Like a tumbleweed blown on the wind, first time you see it there ain't much to notice, but after a while it picks up speed and a little more brush and gets a way bigger. And before you know it, there's a whole peck of tumbleweed blowing your way, and that wind's coming so fierce and strong you can't hardly stand.

The shiver that went through those twenty horses, close together in their makeshift brush corral, was faint as a whisper of breeze through the pine boughs overhead. So faint, none of the soldiers caught it at first. But I've been around horses a while now, and I felt that self-same shiver a heartbeat after. By the time those critters pricked their ears I was rolling for my carbine, knowing we had trouble.

Buford and Conchita were at the edge of the clearing, leading their horses for the nearest stand of pines. They'd just left us a couple of minutes back, aiming to hunt us a mule deer for supper. The scout had his rifle up and levelled for a shot by the time I was on my feet, his sharp eyes scouring the shadowy circle of trees. Conchita, though, saw it first, and pointed to the burst of movement in the pines. We caught a glimpse of a tawny shape that snarled and whipped away uphill through the pine woods, vanishing into tree-shadow before you could take a breath. Quick as Buford was, he couldn't match it for speed. He swore and lowered the Henry, already too late.

'He's away, goddamn him!' Buford said. He turned sideways, spitting into the pine needles and litter at the rim of the clearing. 'Mountain lion, Miss Soledad. You get 'em out here once in a while.'

'Uhuh.' That was what I'd figured. 'Reckon I better go calm the herd, Ike. Leave 'em be, they'll be bustin' loose mighty soon.'

I headed to where the horses milled around inside the brushwood fence, whinnying and shying around in fright. Lion scent was still in their nostrils, and they weren't about to quiet down right away. I talked to them, soft and gentle like always, soothing them the best I could, as Armitage and the others came scrambling over with their carbines hoisted, peering into the trees in that half-scared, half-angry way folks have when they're still trying to figure out what the hell goes on.

'Mountain lion,' I glanced back over my shoulder, patting and stroking the nearest of the fretting horses as I answered. 'He's gone for now, lieutenant. Just spooked the horses a little, is all.'

'Lookin' us over, most like,' Buford called out from the edge of the trees. The scout swung up across his pony, resting the rifle on the animal's neck as Conchita mounted her own horse beside him. 'Don't reckon he'll be back, but keep your eyes peeled. We'll be along with the deer in a while.'

'Now just a minute...' Armitage began, in that tight-assed voice of his. He didn't get to finish. Buford and Conchita touched heels to their mounts and headed into the trees. I left Armitage to smoulder, murmuring to the herd until those twenty horses of mine were calm and quiet again. When I turned around to look, he was still hot enough to fire tinder.

'When that fellow returns, I'll have something to say to him.' Armitage spat out the words like they tasted bad, fixing me with a blue-eyed stare. 'Things are getting far too lax out here, Miss Soledad. Time to enforce some discipline, it seems to me.'

I was set to disagree with him, but Burgin didn't give me the chance.

'Permission to speak, lieutenant,' Burgin saluted sharply, meeting the kid's eye as Armitage swung his way. 'With the lieutenant's permission, it's time we changed the sentries. All right to have Calladine and Treadwell take over now?'

'Of course, sergeant.' Armitage's voice still had kind of a snap to it, like Burgin had caught him out somehow. Like maybe he should have thought of it first, and felt a little sore about it. 'Carry on!'

'Sir!' Burgin jolted to attention, the salute whipping up to the side of his head. That busted crag of rock that served him for a face didn't give away a hint of what he thought as he yelled out to the troopers behind him. 'Calladine! Treadwell! You heard the lieutenant! Pick up them carbines an' git over there, you got the next watch!'

Calladine and Treadwell jumped to it, their carbines at the trail as they headed for the far side of the clearing. Neither one looked like he was about to enjoy himself, but with Burgin giving the orders I figured they weren't in a mood to argue about it.

We'd come up through the foothills, climbing the canyon trails with their covering of chaparral and juniper and cactus stands, into the pine woods at the higher reaches of the mountains. Pines hemmed the clearing on three sides, while on the fourth the trees gave way to a broken, rock-littered slope, that went down through boulders and clumps of brush for the maze of canyons below. An hour or so back, Burgin had detailed Hood and Griffin to a position beyond a boulder outcrop on the right. It was out of sight of the camp but gave a fair view of the woods and gullies around. Now, watching Calladine and Treadwell disappear behind the boulders, I thought about the pair that Burgin had sent out before them. The old man and the kid. Seemed to me if I'd been picking men for a dangerous mission, Hood and Griffin would have been the last fellers on my list. Come to think, most of the others wouldn't have made it either. And knowing that didn't make me feel any better.

Like I say, trouble starts off small, and builds quicker than you know it. If I'd been smart I'd have took that mountain lion as a warning. But I didn't, did I? Could be I'm getting dumber in my old age, feller, but I ain't asking you to nod your head. Instead I sauntered back to where I'd been before, and hunkered down by my saddle-blanket, laying the carbine alongside. After a while Armitage came over and sat beside me. He still didn't look any too pleased.

'See Burgin picked the sentries again,' I said. Guess I might have sounded a little testy myself. 'Seems to me like you listen to that feller a hell of a lot, Mr Armitage.'

I glanced across to where Burgin squatted by his bed-roll and carbine, his back to the pair of us. Wild was with him, lying flat on his blanket with his hands behind his head. My blackstripe dun was tethered to a half-grown shrub away from the rest, and most of the troopers had hobbled their mounts, but Wild had left his critter ground-reined to crop the sparse grass in the clearing. Lucky it hadn't bolted when the lion showed up. Any other time I might have warned him about it, but right now I reckoned I had the lieutenant to deal with.

'It's called delegation, Miss Soledad.' Armitage eyed me like I was a troublesome kid that had to have everything explained real simple. From the sound of his voice, though, I could tell he was losing patience. 'Burgin is an experienced soldier, in case

74

you had failed to notice. He's a veteran Indian fighter, and he knows his way around.'

I looked to Burgin again, but the big sergeant didn't move. Maybe he heard us, and maybe he didn't. He sure as hell gave no sign of it.

'Yeah, an' so does Ike Buford!' Now I was getting more than a little hot under the collar myself. 'How come you don't listen to him so close?'

'Because he's a civilian, and insolent into the bargain!' Armitage flared up like kerosene on corn-shucks, his smooth kid's face reddening. The lieutenant glared at me, his blue eyes fiercer than ever. 'We are grateful for your help, Miss Soledad, but I must ask you not to question my authority. I have been given the command of this mission, and any decisions are my responsibility!'

'Is that right?' You can bet I didn't sound impressed. 'Ask me, Armitage, your sergeant's been runnin' this show from the start, an' he's sure as hell the one them troopers are listenin' to. Tell you somethin' else, feller. This has to be the sorriest bunch of hand-picked men I set eyes on for one heck of a while. An' I get the feelin' that whoever hand-picked them, you didn't have nothin' to do with it!'

'Miss Soledad! That will do!' Armitage looked so hot, I figured he might just burst into flames. The shave-tail started to his feet, dusting down his flashy *vaquero* rig. ' I refuse to discuss the matter further, do you hear?'

From out by the boulders came a dull, muffled thump, and the sound of a smothered cry. Armitage froze as he heard it, then fumbled with the buttoned flap of his holster while I grabbed for my carbine on the ground.

'No need for you to worry, lieutenant,' Burgin said. 'We got everythin' under control.'

He was on his feet looking toward us, and so was the .45 Colt Army pistol that he'd drawn from his holster while the pair of us were still chewing things over. That black muzzle was holding mighty steady on the lieutenant's middle, and from here it looked awful big. Wild was standing too, away to Burgin's left, feet braced wide and teeth bared in that horsey grin as he levelled his carbine on the buckle of my belt. I let go of the Winchester and stayed still as a rock.

'Sergeant?' Armitage still wasn't too sure

what was happening, but the shake in his voice showed he didn't care for it overmuch. 'Sergeant Burgin, what is the meaning of this?'

'Shut your lip an' sit down, Armitage,' Burgin said. The words came out calm and chilly as falling snowflakes. 'Button that holster while you're at it, mister. Best leave the gun where it is, I reckon.'

Now it got through to the shave-tail, and the colour drained from him quicker than paint in a heatwave. He sat down hard on the ground, like he was trying not to fall. For the first time, Burgin smiled, his rocky features breaking open to show strong, yellowish teeth.

'That's better,' the sergeant said. He nodded to where I still hunkered on the ground, the carbine untended beside me. 'Just shove that Winchester away, lady, an' leave it lie.'

I did like he told me, starting to feel kind of sick myself.

'What you just heard was Hood an' Griffin bein' took out,' Burgin said. He held on to that grin, and I have to say it didn't do nothing for me at all. 'They were both of 'em too dumb to buy into this, Armitage. We just brung 'em along for the ride, an' now they're left behind. From here on, it's just the four of us.'

'You mean you've killed them?' Armitage's voice wasn't much more than a croak.

'Not me.' The sergeant shook his head, still grinning tightly. 'Calladine an' Treadwell slugged 'em, an' now they'll be ropin' 'em good. All we have to do is leave 'em for the Apaches once we're gone. That oughta be enough.' He eyes the two of us thoughtfully over the foresight of the pistol. 'You an' the lady here, I ain't so sure...'

'Why are you doing this to us?' Armitage pleaded with him, his face white as a ripped floursack. 'What can you hope to gain?'

Wild broke into a harsh, whinnying laugh and Burgin chuckled and shook his head again, almost like he felt sorry for us. Almost.

'Think about it,' Burgin said. The grin was gone and his voice sounded bitter. 'We go ahead with this damn-fool mission, like as not we git ourselves killed. If we're lucky an' make it back, best I kin look forward to is rottin' away in some stinkin' veterans' home. I been fifteen years in this lousy army, feller, an' not a goddamn thing but my stripes to show for it! Time I had me some payment on account!'

'So what do you aim to do?' I asked. Reckon I knew the answer.

'What the hell you think, lady?' Burgin nodded to where the herd milled around uneasily in its brushwood pen. 'Over there you got twenty good horses goin' to waste. Once we're through with you, we'll be headed for Mexico, we already got a buyer lined up for the deal. Oughta clean up real neat, I reckon.'

'Damn it, Burgin! Listen to me!' Armitage found his voice again, choking on the words. 'This is a woman's life you're throwing away! If Snake doesn't get these horses, she'll be killed!'

'You figure I should cry about it, maybe?' Burgin hawked and spat, his effort landing close to the shave-tail's polished boots. 'No way he's aimin' to turn her loose, an' he'll nail our hides to the wall if he gits the chance. No sense us gittin' ourselves killed on account of some dumb bitch that goes runnin' off to meet the Apache.'

'Don't you dare talk about her that way, you hear!' I figured Armitage was set to bust his strings. He started to stand up again, both fists clenched and white-knuckled, ready to throw himself forward at the gun. Burgin just flipped that pistol barrel an inch or so upward, and the kid let out a shuddering breath, sinking down again.

'Reckon I heard enough from you, Armitage,' the sergeant told him. 'Now lie quiet, an' take your lickin', mister toy soldier.' He shot a sidelong glance to the trooper, nodding his grizzled head. 'Git the ropes, Wild.'

'Why don't we finish 'em now, huh?' Wild spared me a poisonous look. Seemed he hadn't forgotten that business with the horse at the Verde crossing, any more than I had. At the fierce expression on Burgin's face, he went quiet again.

'Just git the ropes, all right?' the sergeant said. He studied us both like he was still thinking it over. 'Ain't yet made up my mind over you an' Miss Soledad here. Could be we'll settle the pair of you now, or maybe we'll leave you for the Injuns to find, along with Hood an' Griffin. Once we got you roped good an' tight, I'll have time to work it out, I guess.'

'Ain't you forgettin' Buford?' I ventured. I figured the longer we kept him talking, the better chance we had. 'Him an' Conchita are gonna be back in a while.'

Wild was crouching on the ground, laying down his carbine as he fumbled in his pockets for the rawhide thongs. The mean grin he gave me, and the look in Burgin's pale eyes, were answer enough.

'Just leave him to me, the half-breed sonofabitch,' Burgin said. And almost as he spoke, the other voice answered.

'Maybe you better tell him about it, soldier,' Ike Buford said.

He edged into sight from our left, where the trees met the first of the rough, bouldery slope. He held the long rifle one-handed, braced in the crook of his arm, leading the Indian pony with his free hand. The rifle fixed on the sergeant as Burgin turned around. A few steps behind him, Conchita led the second pony, a shorter carbine lowered in her grip.

'Drop the gun, Burgin!' The scout's voice bit harder. Buford scanned the nearby rocks warily, suspicion in his black, deep-set eyes. 'Where are the others?'

It was Conchita who called out first, spotting the two men who crouched in the boulders on the right. The warning shout was still in her throat as flame stabbed from the rocks. Ike Buford yelled, stumbling back like he'd been kicked by an army mule. With the bullwhip crack of the carbine shots he pitched down, plunging over the lip of the slope. We watched like we were turned to stone as he ploughed away out of sight in a cloud of dust and flying stones, the rifle slithering after him for the bed of the canyon.

Calladine and Treadwell broke cover, charging through the boulders with their carbines trailing smoke. Conchita was in the saddle as the shots sounded. The Apache woman caught the fallen rope of Buford's mount, kicked heels to run both ponies for the shelter of the trees. Treadwell got off a last shot that was hurried and high, the bullet ripping into pine boughs the way she'd gone. Calladine slid on a loose rock and went down on all fours, cussing as he fought to hang on to his carbine.

Penned in the brush corral, my twenty horses reared and shrilled in fright, struggling to kick a way out as the gunshots spooked them. The troopers' mounts fought their hobbles and my blackstripe dun hauled on his tether in a panic, and I knew we weren't about to get a better chance. Burgin had frozen for the thinnest sliver of a second when Buford went down, Wild still crouching with the rawhide ties in his hand. I grabbed the nearest stone I could find and shied it at the critter he'd left ground-reined, hitting it square on the flank. I have to tell you that stone went sore against my principles, but the way I read it we were already out of choices. The horse squealed as it was hit, and launched itself across the clearing at a run, but I didn't stay around to look. Soon as that critter sang out, I was diving for my .45-70 and working the lever for a shot.

'Let's go, Armitage!' I shouted.

Burgin was swivelling back around and the black muzzle of his Colt was fixing on my belly-button when the horse slammed into him and sent him flying. Wasn't no more than a glancing blow the critter's shoulder caught him in passing, but it was enough. Burgin bounced off the horse's flank and hit the dirt with a racking thud that made me wince to hear it. He lost the pistol, and it slithered across the ground out of reach. I let it lie, running for my horse like the Apaches had just lit a fire in my behind.

Wild reared up ahead, dropping the thongs to grab for his fallen carbine. I triggered on the run and the shot blew up a spray of dirt and stones that stung his face. Wild yelled out and drew back his hand, one arm shielding his face as he stumbled away for cover. I was willing to bet he wasn't grinning now. The horses were screaming and throwing themselves against the brushwood fence, frantic to get clear as the gunshots blasted back and forth across the clearing. I kicked loose a hunk of thorny bush, and the nearest of the herd plunged out from the corral. One of the bay horses led, most of the browns following in a charging, headlong rush. Somewhere beyond them I could hear the yelling voices of Calladine and Treadwell as they started in towards us. I got to where my dun was tethered, and hurried to turn him loose.

'Stand clear, Miss Soledad!' Armitage called.

He had his holster unbuttoned at last, and the .45 pistol was in his hand, wavering around as he looked for a target. He had that dumb hero expression on his face, and that's something that always spells trouble.

'Forget the Custer crud, an' git on over here!' I yelled. I wrenched the halter out of the brush, and grabbed a stirrup to climb aboard. 'We ain't got no time!'

That stupid son didn't move right away, still standing there like he was thinking it over. Then Calladine got off a shot from beyond the horses, the slug whining as it whipped past the shave-tail's head, and Armitage woke up mighty quick. He started running after me, clumsy in his heavy boots, as all hell broke loose around us. By now I was heading back for him at a risky gallop, hung low with my face to the dun's mane and fighting to find my other stirrup while I struggled to hold on to the rein and my Winchester at the same time. The horse herd had scattered for the trees at the end of the clearing, but stalled and turned back once they got there, milling around in a smothering dust-cloud as they blocked us off from Calladine and Treadwell. Burgin was down and out of the fight, rolling clear of those trampling hooves. Wild was into cover, and unarmed. But that was something that could change real soon, and I didn't aim to be around when it happened. No time to free Armitage's mount, or any of the others. Critter I was riding was our one ticket out of here. I got the rein into my teeth, and gripped that dun's barrel like I aimed to squeeze the breath out of him, cradling the Winchester as I reached for Armitage with the hand I had left.

'C'mon, git a hold!' I yelled. 'Up behind me, an' make it fast!' My foot caught in the offside stirrup, and I breathed a touch easier. Armitage grabbed hold, floundering to keep up as the dun forged ahead, and dived for the horse's back. I felt the jolt as he clung on, and wondered if he was about to haul me down. Then he landed astride, and hung on with both arms round my waist. I wrapped the rein around my wrist, and brought the Winchester into both hands as those tall pines came flashing closer.

'Just stay tight!' I told him.

Somewhere from out of that storm of dust and whinnying horseflesh came stabs of flame, and what sounded like a couple of mighty mean hornets went zipping past my head. I swear one touched my neck with the hint of a breeze, and I'm telling you that's plenty close enough! I swung round in the saddle, Armitage pulling me a mite askew as he hung on behind, and squeezed off three or four snap shots of my own, aiming over where I figured the horses' heads would be, and the gunfire stopped. I knew I hadn't a hope in hell of hitting a target in that much dust, but it seemed like we'd discouraged them for the present. We dodged a stray brown from my herd, and hit through the pines at a crazy run that I wouldn't have cared to try any other time. Once we were out of the clearing I stowed the Winchester in the scabbard and gave that blackstripe dun a mighty long rein. Even ridden double, he went like a Union Pacific locomotive aiming at record time. The way them pines flicked past us turned me dizzy, and I tried not to think too hard about gopher holes. Maybe I prayed a little, I reckon it's been known. For once we stayed lucky. The dun didn't break a leg, and Armitage and me didn't break our necks. After a while the critter began to tire and I eased him down, shortening rein gradually until he steadied to a stroll. By then we were quite a distance from that clearing, and there was no sign of them coming after.

'Why are we running from them?' Armitage wanted to know. From the time I'd called out to him he hadn't opened his mouth, staying quiet as a mouse. Hearing him now, I figured I'd liked him better that way.

''Cause they're four agin two, goddamn it!' I cut back at him, my voice as sharp as I could make it. 'I got news for you, Armitage. You ain't General Custer, an' we ain't about to git ourselves massacred. You reckon you kin follow that?'

Tell truth, I was sore about plenty of things right then. Leaving my horses running loose was bad enough. Scared as they were, the critters might fall and bust a leg, or stop a bullet from Treadwell or Calladine. There was the thought of what had happened to Ike Buford, and Conchita alone and in danger. And worst of all, here was I riding double with Mr Shave-tail Hero himself in the middle of Apache country, and everybody after our blood. Thinking it over, it wasn't too surprising I took things kind of hard. And just like I figured, Armitage didn't turn a hair.

'If you insist.' The kid didn't sound too sure. He still held tight to me around the waist, more than he needed, it seemed to me. 'Personally, I'd have been inclined to shoot it out with those scoundrels. The trouble is, with women like yourself and the Apache female around, it's difficult to risk a fight.'

'Is that right?' The words came out like they'd just been doused in coal-oil. Lucky for him I couldn't turn around, or he might have died right then and there. 'Maybe you should've mentioned it before, Armitage. I might just have stayed home! Who was it just pulled off that rescue job back there, mister? Answer me that!'

'Well now,' he offered. 'I'd say it was really

the scouts who gave us the chance.'

'Yeah, that's right!' He sure knew how to get me riled, and that was a fact. 'Ike Buford, an' that Apache woman you been talkin' about! Now Buford's dead, she's on the run an' so are we! All on account of you bein' fooled by that lousy Sergeant Burgin of yours! You'd have done better listenin' to Buford, an' that's the truth!'

I reckoned I'd let off all the steam I needed by then, and began to simmer down a little. Guess I'd made the point with Armitage this time around. It was quite a spell before he answered, and when he did he was way less sharp than he'd been before.

'You're right, of course,' the lieutenant admitted. 'It appears I misjudged them both. Who would have thought a man like Burgin would take to horse theft and murder, after years in the service?' He sighed, still holding on as the horse took us ahead. 'Do you think they'll follow us now?'

'Not for a while,' I told him. 'When we left, they'd still to get their horses un-hobbled. Them fellers ain't horse-herders, an' with four of 'em to twenty scared horses they'll have their hands full. Fun starts later, when they get the herd back together.'

'What do you mean, exactly?' He was slow

to get the message.

'It's this way, Armitage,' I told him. 'We have to go back an' git them horses, or there ain't no deal with Serpiente.'

'To be sure, Miss Soledad. It's why we came here.' He was back sounding brisk and spry again. 'Anything less, and Miss Mansfield's life is in danger.'

'Right now it's you an' me I'm thinkin' about,' I told him. 'Snake catches us out here without the horses, wouldn't give a bent dime for our chances. Now if you'd oblige me, I'd breathe easier if you let go an' stepped down from the horse. He's gonna founder if we ride him double all the way.'

He went real quiet then, and I reckoned I felt him blush up hot all the way through the back of my shirt. Armitage eased his grip on me, and slid down the flank of the dun to the ground. Way he looked up at me, I got the feeling he was a mite unhappy about how it was going.

'We take turns to walk an' ride,' I said. 'An' he's my horse, so I ride him first. That's fair enough, ain't it?'

'If you say so, Miss Soledad,' Armitage muttered, still puzzled. 'Tell me, how do you intend that we recapture the herd, when we've run from them already?'

90

'That I've still to figure,' I told him.

No way I was looking forward to it, that was for sure. Burgin on his own was likely to be hard enough, and to go up against four soldiers with carbines and pistols was the next best thing to suicide. If we were going to get those horses back, we'd have to get the drop somehow. And even then, I'd have been happier with a couple more guns along to back us up. But beggars can't be choosers.

By the time we came out of the pine woods, heading along a canyon whose sides were choked with boulders and brush, it had begun to get dark, and the first stars were blinking out overhead like sunlight off a spur. I rode the dun at a slow walk, Armitage stumbling alongside in his horseman's boots and panting a little when he hit an upturned rock here and there. We were a mile or so along the canyon when something moved in the scrub by the trail, and another figure came staggering out.

'Please,' the voice begged. 'Please, you have to help me...'

I'd reached for the Winchester when the first move came, but quit when I heard her speak. Now I could see what we'd stumbled on, right enough. A tall, high-bosomed female with a pale, freckled face and bright red hair. That hair was matted into her eyes, and the fancy riding-habit that fitted her tight as a second skin was ripped and tattered by the thorn brush and spattered with mud, but she was one hell of a looker for all that. And if she surprised me, that was nothing to what she did for Armitage. The shave-tail froze like he'd stepped into an iceberg, eyes staring wide as he took her in.

'Lydia!' The kid gasped out the word. Catching the look she gave him, he swallowed hard. 'Miss Mansfield! How do you come to be here?'

And now I reckoned I really knew what trouble was. Two to a horse, Apaches all around, and now it looked like the canary had bust its cage and flown right here to meet us.

'Lady,' I told her. 'You're surely welcome, but right now I reckon we could use a little help ourselves. An' from what I kin see, it's about to git a whole sight worse.'

I swung out of my stirrups, and stepped down from the horse, letting the poor critter stand. Way I saw it, we'd both of us earned the rest. And maybe we wouldn't get another chance this side of the cemetery gates.

FIVE

'So how'd you get away from Snake?' I wanted to know.

I sat with my back to the nearest of the rocks, my shoulders resting easy on the stone. By now we'd reached a second gully a mile or so from the first, and were all pretty well worn out. Armitage slumped, hands on his knees, staring at Miss Mansfield like he'd never set eyes on her before. Just what it was with the two of them I wasn't too sure, but I reckoned I was beginning to get there. As for the lady, she didn't seem anything like as worried as she'd been when we met up with her the first time, as she leaned back on the rock behind her and patted that pretty red hair into place.

'As it happened, it wasn't too difficult,' Lydia said. She smiled across at me, not a friendly smile exactly, more like she figured it might be tough for me to understand. This close, I saw her eyes were green and sharp as glass, and they went real well with that milky skin and red hair. I was willing to bet she knew it, too. 'They were camped in the mountains, on top of a mesa. Three nights ago we had a bad storm, with thunder and heavy rain. The Apaches kept a big pony herd in the camp, and the lightning must have panicked them. They broke out all over the mesa and Snake and his people had trouble rounding them up.' She paused, looking me over while she let it sink in. 'That's when I made my escape.'

'Uhuh,' I looked her over, returning the favour. Miss Mansfield was slim and tall, pretty much the same height as me, which is tall for a female let me tell you. That riding-habit of hers looked to be some kind of black velvet stuff that came mighty expensive, and it was messed up real good, smeared and wet with mud-stains and the cloth slashed from the brush she'd been tracking her way through. Same went for her boots, and there were mud specks on her face too, but that didn't take nothing from her. She was a looker, and no mistake. 'How'd that happen?'

'Everyone went to catch the horses, they left me alone in one of those shelters.'

'Wickiup you mean?'

'I believe that's what they're called.' Lydia's smile tightened up a notch. 'They hadn't bound my hands or feet so it was a simple matter to slip out while the storm was keeping them busy. The rain was so hard I could barely see, but I expect the same was true for them. I started down the side of the *mesa*, but all the trails were flooded, it was like wading through rivers. One of the trails I found, the floodwater carried me with it. I had to swim for my life.'

'Good heavens!' Armitage still stared at her in that dumb-ox kind of way as he spoke. 'To think of you, alone and in such danger!'

'I'm here, aren't I?' Lydia turned to me, the mean smile coming back. 'Fortunately I can swim, Miss Soledad, but even so I had to go with the current for some distance. After a while it slowed, and I was able to scramble to land. By then I was well clear of the Apache camp. Since then I have worked my way down from the mountains on foot as best I can, lying low to avoid discovery. Until I met the two of you, that is.'

'Lydia...' Catching her eye, Armitage gulped and corrected himself. 'Miss Mansfield, that was magnificent! Your courage is surely an example to us all.' He broke off, frowning as he struggled to get out the words he wanted. 'Tell me, Miss Mansfield.

Did they? Did they ... harm you?'

At the mocking smile she gave him his face went real hot, and he looked down at his boots.

'You know what he means, girl,' I said.

'Of course not!' She sighed, shaking her head. 'That savage Snake wants his horses, doesn't he? To him, I don't count so much.' Glancing at the flushing shave-tail, she chuckled. 'Besides, do you think I'd tell you if he did?'

At that Armitage looked ready to burst into tears, and I reckoned I did have the picture. Trouble was, Lydia was starting to raise my hackles just a little. Sure, she'd been through plenty here in the Mogollons, and you didn't need tellling she had sand, but something about that lady sure rubbed me raw. Maybe it was the thought of Ike Buford lying in some canyon bed, or Conchita on the run. Or those poor bastards Hood and Griffin, trussed up and waiting for Snake to find them. Seemed to me they were all down to Lydia, and if we weren't real careful we could be next. After that, to hear her talk to Armitage that was more than I could stand.

'Just give the feller a break, all right?' I said. 'He came out here to help you.'

'Really?' Lydia laughed, her pale face scornful. She ran a cold glance over Armitage, who looked more miserable than before. 'Imagine, Sterling Armitage, my would-be rescuer! I presume this is what they mean by sending a boy to do a man's job?'

'No one sent me, Lydia.' The kid sounded hurt. 'As soon as I learned of your predicament, I volunteered. Believe me, I'm delighted to see you safe.'

'Just as well I escaped, though, wasn't it?' Lydia cut a sharp glance from him to me, and on to the blackstripe dun that stood cropping the sparse grass beyond. 'If this is the best the army can manage, Snake has nothing to fear. Where are the twenty horses that were my ransom, if you don't mind me asking?'

Now Armitage began to look mighty uncomfortable, and I felt the urge to get hold of Lydia and shake that smart little smile off her face.

'We've encountered a number of problems,' the lieutenant admitted. 'At present the horses are in other hands, and we're rather outgunned, but hopefully matters will improve shortly.' He paused, his voice growing gentler. 'Miss Mansfield, your father Colonel Thornhill organized this expedition on your behalf, and called on Miss Soledad here for the horses. He's extremely worried about your safety.'

'I'd be grateful if you didn't mention Colonel Thornhill to me, Mr Armitage.' Lydia's voice was cold as a Montana winter. 'And may I remind you he is not my father, merely the second husband of my widowed mother. Believe it or not, there is a difference.'

'Seems to me you're singin' a different tune from what we heard back in that canyon, lady,' I said. I met that cold stare of hers head-on, so she knew I meant business. 'Let me tell you, Miss Mansfield, I ain't here on account of my health, an' you just brung us more trouble than we need. Pretty soon Snake's gonna be out lookin' for you, an' when he finds us he ain't gonna be happy. Tell you somethin' else, if you reckon we're dumb, ain't nothin' comes dumber than what you been doin', runnin' round the Mogollon Rim all on your lonesome an' getting' took off by the Apaches. Just what the hell got into you, girl?'

I saw her face tighten up, and I swear she went a shade whiter. For maybe half a second she was on her heels, but being

Lydia she blazed right back again.

'My presence here is none of your business!' Lydia snapped. 'How dare you speak to me in that way!' She struggled to get to her feet. The riding-habit didn't help any, tight as it was. 'Believe me, if I were not a lady...'

'Don't you worry none over that,' I said. I got up easily and stood, ready for whatever might be coming. 'You want to make somethin' of it, Lydia girl, you go right ahead. Just be sure you take your best shot first; all right?'

'Miss Soledad!' Armitage thrust in between us, holding us apart the best he could. 'Lydia, please! This is no way to behave!'

Lydia was struggling to get past him, and he was having trouble holding her back, and I sure as hell wasn't about to move. We were all set for a knock-down drag-out brawl when that dun horse pricked his ears and blew down his nose, and I knew right away we had more important things to deal with.

'This is gonna have to keep, Lydia,' I said. I leaned sideways to snatch up my .45-70 from where it leaned by the rock in easy reach. 'Let her go, Armitage, an' git that holster unbuttoned. You an' me got work to do.'

Sound of my voice was enough to make him loosen his hold, and Lydia tugged free, still glaring and breathing hard. Armitage looked ready to argue for a moment, but I guess he saw I wasn't fooling. He flipped the holster open, and got the pistol clear.

'Into the boulders yonder,' I told him. 'An' be ready to use it. Lady, best get to cover an' stay low. This could get a little rough.'

I led the dun deeper into cover and roped him to a thorn bush, and the three of us ducked into the boulders as fast as we could. That horse had good ears, all right. We'd waited barely a half-hour when the clip of hooves carried to us, and soon after that two riders eased out around the bend in the trail and came on for our hiding-place in the rocks, plodding their horses through the dust in a slow, lazy-paced walk. They were almost underneath us when the first horse shied and snorted, dragging its head up against the rein, and the gaunt *hombre* who rode it stiffened and reached down for the gun at his hip.

'Don't even think about it, mister,' I said. I levelled the Winchester over the top of the boulder, the foresight on his chest. To my left came the solid click as the hammer on Armitage's pistol eased to half-cock. 'This here's a .45-70 Winchester, an' it's pointed your way. My friend has your friend covered too. Seems to me we got the edge on you here.'

'What you want from us, lady?' the second one asked. He was shorter and thickset, his voice gruffer than his friend's. Both men peered up into the rocks, trying to work out what they were up against.

'Just come on up,' I told them. 'Once you're here, get down from your horses an' stay put. An' no funny moves, okay? I could pick out a buzzard's eye from where I'm stood right now.'

'Anythin' you say, lady,' the gaunt feller answered. He and the short one turned off the trail, coming up slow and steady through the rocks and brush to where we stood waiting. Once inside the circle of boulders they dismounted, letting the ropes of their horses drop to the ground.

'So what happens now?' The taller one let his glance run over me real slow, like he wanted to be sure he had it right. He was six feet high and stoop-shouldered, with a gaunt, hollow-cheeked face and a chin that disappeared almost out of sight. His eyes were watery and pale, overset by bristling brows, and his big jug-ears were thick with undergrowth of their own. When he opened his mouth I saw he hadn't a tooth in his head. 'What you got in mind for us, lady?'

'You got it right there, mister,' I told him. 'This here's a female, even if she does rig out like a man. Now if you're through lookin' me over an' getting' ideas you'd be better off without, maybe I'll tell you.'

That wizened, leathery face flushed up hot and red, and for an instant he looked ready to rush me. Guess the muzzle of the Winchester lined on his belly was enough to change his mind.

'No offence, ma'am.' He tugged off his battered range hat, showing me a head as bald and smooth as a thumb. He was the nearest thing I'd seen to a turtle, and no mistake. 'Best we should introduce ourselves, I guess. Name's Mose Hargreaves, an' this here's my pardner Vern Copestake. We're cattle ranchers, back in Pleasant Valley.'

He flapped the ragged apology for a hat at the second man, who stood staring my way with a face as grim as the Day of Judgement.

'Pleased to meet you, lady,' Copestake

didn't sound like he meant it.

He was short and barrel-chested, wide as a door and showing about as much in the way of feeling. His eyes were a dull grey, and most of his face was hidden by thick ginger sideburns and moustache that joined up to give it cover. From here, it looked like he was peering at me through a thicket. Like Hargreaves, he was rigged in a filthy plaid shirt and threadbare Levis, his hat showing a brim so ragged I figured the dogs must have chewed it over. They had to be the sorriest pair of cattle ranchers I'd set eyes on.

'So tell me how come you're out here,' I said. 'This is a fair ride out from Pleasant Valley, seems to me.'

The bald feller stooped a little lower, those watery eyes small and pebble-hard as his brows pulled together. He was still working at an answer when the shave-tail cut in from behind me.

'If you don't mind, Miss Soledad,' Armitage didn't hide his impatience. He laid a hand on the barrel of my carbine, easing it down, and smiled. 'I'm Sterling Armitage, gentlemen. Pleased to make your acquaintance. Sight of white men is extremely welcome in these parts. This lady is Miss Lydia Mansfield, and I believe you have already met Miss Soledad.'

'Yeah, reckon we have, at that,' Copestake muttered. Meantime, Hargreaves had switched his look to Lydia, and the way his eyes lit up told a story all by itself.

'Well, ma'am, this surely is a pleasure.' The gaunt feller caught her hand in his bony claws, and gripped it like he didn't want to let go too quick. 'Sure didn't figure on meetin' anyone this pretty out here, if you don't mind me sayin'.'

'You're too kind, Mr Hargreaves.' Lydia forced a frosty smile, breaking his grip with an effort. Armitage glared at me kind of fierce, and I lowered the carbine.

'You were about to tell us how you came to be here, I believe?' Lydia's smile didn't fit the sharpness in her voice. She might have said more, only Armitage cut in again.

'Perhaps we can sit down and talk this over in a civilized fashion,' the kid offered. The look he gave me and Lydia, though, was anything but kind. 'Mr Hargreaves and Mr Copestake will be happy to explain, I'm sure.'

'Be glad to, Armitage,' Hargreaves' turtle-face puckered in a toothless grin.

'Maybe we oughta cut some brush, fix

ourselves a fire,' Copestake put in. 'Got coffee an' sweetenin' back in my saddle-bags yonder.'

The gaunt feller shot him a look so venomous it would have choked a side-winder, and Copestake went quiet in an instant.

'Best we don't do that, I reckon,' Hargreaves' smile had vanished, his leathery face grown serious. 'This here's Apache country. No sense in raisin' a ruckus cuttin' brush an' sendin' up smoke to bring 'em in close.' He paused, heading back for where his horse stood ground-reined behind him. 'Now if it's whisky you're talkin' about, got me a bottle right here you might care to try.'

Armitage and Lydia settled down, squatting in the open ground beyond the boulsders overlooking the trail. I stayed watching, ready for any cute moves as Hargreaves reached into his saddle-bags. Once he pulled out the bottle I let him be and went over to the dun, reaching down my canteen and a couple of strips of sun-dried beef I had fixed under the saddle. Pretty soon the five of us were seated, and passing around what food and drink we had to spare.

'Well now, this is mighty festive, I reckon,' Hargreaves cracked that toothless turtle grin, holding out the bottle. 'You care for a taste, Armitage?'

'Thank you, no.' The lieutenant kept that tight, unsure smile. 'I took the pledge some years ago. No offence, you understand.'

'Sure, Armitage. None taken.' Hargreaves peered my way from under those thick, bushy brows. 'How 'bout you, Miss Soledad?'

'Guess not,' I told him. 'Thanks all the same.'

I unstopped my flask and took a drink. Water was tepid, and its taste mixed with the leather and metal of the canteen, but I figured it was welcome. When Hargreaves offered the bottle to Lydia she smiled and shook her head.

'OK, folks. Have it your way.' He hoisted the bottle and drank, his throat with its bobbing Adam's apple working overtime. Liquor in that bottle was yellow and ugly and put me in mind of something that had just passed through a horse, but it didn't seem to spoil his fun. The gaunt man took two or three slugs before breathing out hard and letting go. Hargreaves wiped the top with a filthy sleeve and shoved the bottle across to his friend.

'That's better.' He leaned back contentedly, covering his mouth as the air came back in a hurry. 'You was askin' what we were doin' here, right? Well, fact is, our ranch was raided a week back by a bunch of Apaches. They run off thirty head, an' we come out here to hunt for 'em, maybe git 'em back.'

'Just the two of you, Mr Hargreaves?' Lydia sure knew how to put a barb into her voice. 'I'd have thought that was rather dangerous.'

'Bless you, lady. We ain't that dumb.' The bald feller bared toothless gums, shaking his boulder-smooth head. 'Was eight of us set off, but first one feller's hoss went lame, an' a couple of the others turned back. Five of us still on their trail, tracked 'em into the foothills yonder before we lost 'em. Vern an' me left the others to wait an' rid on here, figurin' we might just cut 'em off before they got away.'

'Didn't work out though, Mose,' Copestake muttered. It was kind of hard to tell what he said, on account of the bottle in his mouth.

'Guess not, pardner,' Hargreaves sounded rueful. Seeing I was offering him a strip of jerked beef, he grinned again, reaching over to grab it. 'Thanks, lady. That's mighty kind.' He dug in the pocket of his Levis and hauled out a grimy bandanna, opening it up. I found myself studying a full set of false teeth that stared right back at me. 'Now, if you ladies will excuse me.'

The three of us watched as he fitted the dentures into his mouth, and took hold on that hunk of meat. This time the grin he gave us was even scarier, and from what I could see those teeth didn't fit him any too well.

'Got 'em from a dentist with a medicine show in Albuquerque, 'bout a year back.' Hargreaves grinned and bit into the meat, tearing at it like an alligator snapper. 'Reckon they're right handy when it comes time to eat.'

Lydia and Armitage didn't say a word, shocked into silence. As for Copestake, he was too busy getting to the bottom of that bottle to notice.

I looked the two of them over, and still wasn't sure. Can't say I ever bought that line about them being cattle ranchers, the way Armitage had. They both had the look of saddle-bums at best. But I didn't have them figured for hardcases either. Hargreaves looked close to sixty years old, and Copestake had to be forty-five if he was a day. Pistols they carried were mighty old and worn, and if they made unlikely ranchers they looked even sorrier as gun-hawks. That's what I thought, anyhow. How come we're always dumbest when we ought to be smart? Ain't never figured that.

Lydia was frowning, peering from one to the other as they ate and drank.

'I feel sure I remember seeing you before, Mr Hargreaves,' the redhead decided. She studied him more closely, still frowning. 'Could we have met somewhere, do you think?'

'That could be, lady.' Hargreaves bared those false teeth in a grin that would have done justice to a lobo wolf. 'Me an' Vern here, we been around most places in our time.'

He had the pistol from his belt that same instant, the gun whipping up and drawing level fast as a rattler's strike. It was an old Starr Arms that must have seen action in the '60s, but that black muzzle was lined on my chest before any of us could move. Copestake wasn't far behind, his gun covering Armitage while we were still catching our breath.

'Miss Lydia Mansfield, huh?' Hargreaves grinned, but there wasn't an ounce of kindliness in his leathery face. He slapped the hat on his gleaming skull, and opened his mouth to let the dentures fall on the open bandanna. He had real nice manners, and no mistake. 'Your daddy's Colonel Thornhill, ain't he? Reckon you'd better come with us, little lady.'

'Leave her alone, you hear?' Armitage had a bad case of the Custers again. The kid dived in at Hargreaves, fumbling with that damned button holster as he went. Copestake ducked in and whipped his pistol sideways, like a feller that knew his job. The barrel slammed Armitage across the side of the head and he went down buffaloed, falling like a log. The thickset *hombre* had the gun back in line and pointing my way before I reached the carbine alongside.

'Set it down, bitch!' Copestake said. His gruff voice had a vicious sound. Hargreaves stowed the false teeth in the bandanna, and shoved it back in his pocket. Then he stepped over to where Lydia stood like she'd been frozen into stone.

'Truth is, we didn't come here lookin' for nothin', Miss Mansfield,' the bald feller said. 'Reckon we found us somethin' all the same. Once word gits to your daddy how things stand, he's gonna pay plenty to git you back. Ain't that right?'

'Don't you dare touch me!' Lydia began. Hargreaves paid no mind, cracking his toothless grin as he moved in closer. She lashed out at him, and he hooked his arm around her neck. Lydia fought and kicked, but no way could she get loose. Hargreaves was stronger than he looked. Meaner too.

Armitage was sleeping sound, his hat caved in and hiding his face. I looked into the muzzle of Copestake's gun, and the dull eyes in that thickset of sideburns and moustache. There was nothing on offer from either one.

'Now you we don't need, Miss Soledad.' Hargreaves edged back towards the horses, the big Starr pistol levelled around Lydia's pleasing frame. 'You had plenty to say a while back. Reckon it's time we shut your mouth.'

He nodded to Copestake, and the stocky *hombre* raised that pistol real slow and steady, like he didn't aim to miss. I got to feeling mighty queasy and cold all in one, and pretty soon I was wondering which way that beef was going to come out from me the quickest. Not that it was likely to matter too much.

'Hell, Mose!' Copestake said.

I heard the shock in his voice, caught the sudden scared look that threatened in those cold eyes. Then that ragged-brimmed hat of his took off flying from his head, uncovering a shock of ginger hair as it went. Flat, cracking blast of the rifle carried to me as the hat bounced in the dirt. Dust geysered up by Hargreaves' boots, and a second whiplash noise bit at my ears. Then both of them were going backwards for their horses, the tall *hombre* dragging Lydia with him.

'Come back here, damn it!' I yelled.

I rolled towards the Winchester, and Copestake triggered on the run. Lucky for me he didn't stop to shoot, but it ain't easy to kill somebody while you're running backwards scared to hell. The bullet ripped past my head and into the dirt, making a real mean whistle as it went. I rolled on my belly as the gunblast hammered my ears again, bringing up the Winchester for a shot of my own. I wasn't quick enough. They were up across their horses, Hargreaves holding Lydia between him and the carbine. The pair of them hit the trail at a gallop, firing back over the rumps of their mounts. Fresh shots cracked behind me as I swore and worked the lever, too late again. Dirt flew up short of the two horsemen, then they were away down the trail in a rising shroud of dust, noise of their hoof-beats fading.

'Goddamn it to hell,' I said. I got up slowly, dusting myself off and flinching a little from the bruises I'd taken. Behind me came the clip of other hooves on the stones, and I turned to see Ike Buford and Conchita step out from the far boulders and head towards me, both leading their ponies. Buford shouldered the Henry, and she carried her carbine, both weapons trailing smoke. Seemed to me Burford moved slower than Conchita, treading real careful on the loose crumbs of rock underfoot. Pretty soon they came up to where I stood waiting.

'No, lady,' the scout said. He took a sharp breath with the words, like the talking pained him. 'I ain't dead. Not yet, anyhow.'

'Damn it, I saw them shoot you,' I said. Guess I still wasn't thinking straight. Ike Buford tried the feeblest grin I've ever seen cross a human face, and sat down with his back to the nearest boulder. He let go the rope, and it fell to trail in the dirt.

'Scraped me 'cross the chest, is all.' Buford had trouble answering, his features tight and clenched. 'Ain't no more'n a

113

scratch, I reckon.'

He fell quiet, breathing hard as he settled against the rock. I saw the torn strips from his flannel undershirt that bulked under the buckskin, and bit my lip.

'Good to see you, anyhow,' I told him. 'Thanks, Ike. You too, Conchita.'

The Apache woman didn't answer, her dark face troubled as she looked to Buford sprawled against the boulder. Figuring she didn't understand me, I tried again in Spanish.

'*Habla usted español?*'

'Yes,' Conchita said. 'I speak English too.'

She turned back to me, and this time she smiled. Did me good to see that grin I can tell you, even if the laugh was on me.

'Hell, I'm sorry,' I said. Then, still puzzled. 'How'd you find him?'

'I rode into the woods a short way, and circled back around.' Conchita weighed the carbine on her palms as she answered, the brief smile fading quickly. 'Buford was in the gully bed, his rifle fell with him. He had bruises, but nothing was broken. I got him clear, and saw to his wound. Since then, we have followed your tracks to this place.'

'Burgin an' the others didn't see you go?'

'They were too busy with the herd.' Her

voice showed she didn't rate Burgin and his pals too high. 'They know nothing of horses.'

'An' Hood an' Griffin? The ones they took out?'

'I did not see them.'

'Uhuh.' I let it go. Right now, seemed like neither of us had the answers. One sure thing, she and Buford had done a damn sight better than we had. 'Good thing you showed up when you did, we'd be crow bait otherwise.'

'That her? The one they took off with?' Buford grimaced as he fought out the words. Meeting his pain-wracked face, I nodded.

'Sure, that's her. Lydia Mansfield, the one we come out here to find.' Guess the bitterness showed in my voice. 'Seems she got clear of the Apaches while a storm was on. Now it looks like she might be in worse company.'

Away to the side, Armitage moaned and hauled himself up, staggering to his feet. Pistol barrel made a red, swollen welt across the side of his head, and his face was white as death. He stumbled towards us, blond hair spilling into his eyes as he fumbled with that damned holster of his.

'Lydia!' Armitage reeled, fighting the holster and losing again. 'Those devils, they've taken her! We have to get her back!'

He lurched and slipped backwards, losing his footing on the stones. I got there in time to catch him and lower him to the ground.

'Sure, Armitage,' I told him. 'You've been a real help, all the way along.'

He didn't hear me, head slipping sideways as he groaned and passed out again. Still and all, I felt a mite ashamed. Guess he couldn't help being a dumb lovestruck shave-tail, at that. Right now I was a way madder at myself for having been fooled so easy the second time around. Reckon I was old enough to know better. Then too, I figure I was still getting used to not being dead.

'He ain't goin' nowhere,' Ike Buford said. He caught his breath between the words, laying a hand on the bloody bandages round his chest. The scout fixed me with his dark, piercing eyes, like he needed me to know. 'Can't go after her neither, Miss Soledad. First off, we have to get back them horses.'

'Like hell we do, Ike!' I was boiling mad by now, better believe it. 'Sure, we need the horses, I know that, but there ain't no way I aim to let those bastards take her! She could end up dead, damn it!' I took a breath, giving myself a chance to simmer down, but it didn't help too much. 'Soon as Armitage comes round again, we're gonna get after 'em. OK?'

Buford sighed and shut his eyes for a second or two. When he opened them he tried for that feeble smile again, and almost made it.

'So who put you in charge here, lady?' the Seminole wanted to know.

'You see anybody else?' I said.

Buford shook his head and laughed. Leastways, I figure that's what he did. Take it from me, chuckles don't come no fainter than what I heard.

'OK, general,' the Seminole told me. 'Have it your way.' He smiled again, the pain showing in his face as he made the move. 'Pretty soon, though, we're gonna need them horses.'

'You got it, Ike,' I said. 'Once you an' Armitage are ready to ride, we'd best be gone from here.'

At least the odds were better, I thought. We had three rifles, and three horses between four. And after being twice at the wrong end of the gun, I was sure as hell ready to turn that game around.

I picked up my canteen from the dirt and laid the Winchester on my shoulder, making for where the blackstripe dun stood tethered.

SIX

So we took off after them, just like I wanted. Not that it happened right away, mind. It was an hour and more before Armitage was fit to ride, and even then I figured he wasn't likely to be too much use to us. Then again, feeling about Lydia the way he did I didn't have to talk him around. The shave-tail was just as keen as I was to run those oldsters down. I wasn't too sure about Ike Buford, either, but the scout laughed it off like always. All the same, I couldn't help but see the wry face he pulled when he heaved himself into the saddle. Conchita took Armitage up behind her on the pony she was riding, and that's the way we left the clearing and started following those tracks.

Sure, mister. No need for you to tell me we were loco even to try it, but you hadn't been stood where I had, facing the business end of a pistol and getting ready to die. Hargreaves and Copestake had fooled me good, scared me to hell and back and snatched Lydia Mansfield from right under my nose. Once I got over being terrified, I was mad enough to rip the head off a four hundred pound grizzly bear, and couldn't wait to get my hands on the two old goats who'd caused me such pain. Looking back, I can see I was way too sore to be thinking straight, but that's something that can take a while to figure out. And back then, guess I wasn't in the mood to notice.

Once we were started, it didn't take us long to pick up on the sign they'd left behind. Seemed like those two old sinners hadn't counted on us trailing them at all, and the tracks they put down were plain enough for a five-year-old kid to follow. Armitage wouldn't have had no trouble reading them all by himself let alone with scouts like Buford and Conchita to hand. I studied those two sets of hoofprints in the dirt ahead, and I guess that grin of mine could have looked kind of unpleasant. I was beginning to feel better already.

'Looks like they figure we've given up on them,' I said. I patted the butt of the .45-70 carbine that nestled in its leather scabbard by my right thigh, like I had my hand on their necks this minute. 'Reckon they're gonna find out different, and soon.'

'Yeah, maybe so.' Buford sounded like he wasn't too sure. The scout scanned the canyons and ridges around for signs of movement, his dark leathery face grown thoughtful. Armitage didn't say a word, just touched a hand real careful to the side of his head where that pistol barrel had slugged him, and puckered up his face as the pain answered back. I looked across to Conchita, but even she wasn't smiling this time.

'Well, that's the way I see it, anyhow,' I told them.

Somehow, though, I got the feeling that they still didn't believe me.

We kept on after the tracks of those two horses, and they led us right along, back into those canyons and arroyos we'd come to know so well. You could see from the way the hooves of Hargreaves' mount went into the dirt that he was still riding double with Lydia, and I figured they weren't likely to be making any better time than the four of us. Sooner or later, we had to catch up with them.

After a while we found ourselves at the entrance to a gully whose red rock walls towered up mighty high and sheer on either side to throw it into shadow. I reined in as we reached it, peering into the gloom ahead and checking out the sign on the ground. No doubt about it, those hoofprints went right on in, waiting for us to follow.

'That's the way they went,' I said at last. I slid the Winchester from its sheath and checked the action, just in case. 'If you folks are ready, reckon that's the way we'll be headed too.'

'Shortest way, right enough,' Buford offered. He took his time to say it, and when he did it was like every word pained him. Eyeing him closer, I saw his dark face had gone a sickly, greyish shade, the leathery skin gleaming with sweat. Ike was suffering pretty bad and no mistake. Any time but this, and I'd have counted him out of the game. Now he shaded his eyes, searching the canyons and the forested heights beyond. 'I figure they're aimin' to lair up in that timbered stretch yonder, an' this is the one road through. Any other trail is gonna cost 'em half a day in circlin' round the canyons.' He paused, the dark gaze coming back to me again. 'Goes for us too, I reckon.'

He forced a grin, brushing at the sweat on

his face, and drew an unsteady breath. Beside him Conchita stayed quiet, but there was no hiding the worried look she gave him. Armitage didn't seem like he was up to words at all, still grimacing as he rubbed his head. I peered into that gully again, and figured we'd hung around long enough.

'You said it, Ike,' I told him. 'This is the one way in, if we're gonna find 'em. Let's go, OK?'

No one else answered and I nudged my dun horse forward, stepping into the gully at an easy walk. Behind me I could hear the clip of hooves on rock and the click of the shave-tail's gunhammer as the rest of them followed. Dark of the gully swallowed us right away, the narrow bed of loose stones and boulders and stunted light-starved brush plunged into a deep blue-grey shadow that covered us as we rode. I tried craning my neck to look up at those tall rock walls that hemmed us in on either side, but after a while I had to quit. They were so high, and the dark that came down from them so thick and blanketing, that there was no way that a feller could see clear to the top. I let the dun take me ahead, picking his way warily through the rocks underfoot as the others came on after me. Right now the shadow lay so deep it was hard to make out a goddamn thing, and the rocky ground didn't leave much in the way of sign. Edging along between those high rock cliffs, lining the Winchester to point in front, I found myself hoping we'd be out of here soon.

I didn't have long to wait. Maybe twenty yards further ahead the gully took a tight bend, and as me and the dun eased around that corner in the rock, a blast of sunlight hit through to dazzle us both. Shielding my eyes, I saw the gully widen, the high cliffs giving out to gentler flanking slopes studded with cacti, boulders and thorny brush. Further on, the side walls closed in again, the gully mouth shrinking to a gap wide enough for riders to pass in single file. I tugged my hat brim lower against the glare, and touched heels to my horse's flanks to move him forward. I'd begun to spot fresh hoofprints in the dirt when the blackstripe dun tightened under me, head swinging sideways as his ears went up, and I knew for sure we had trouble.

'Look out ahead!' I shouted. I was down from the horse and searching for a target before the words were out. All the same, it wasn't fast enough. Following the dun's jerking head, I caught the sudden movement on the crest to our right as a single massive boulder leaned over and came bounding down for the gully mouth, smashing into the rocks and brush below it. All at once the stillness was gone, closed space of the ravine booming and echoing to the noise of tumbling rock as that boulder set off a landslide all of its own.

It was as if that hillside slipped its coat the way a rattler shucks off its skin, and the whole of the slope came ploughing down towards us in a flooding rush of boulders, small trees and dirt, throwing up a billowing dust-cloud as it moved. For a while I reckoned we were all of us due to be buried over our heads, but I guess we were luckier than any of us deserved. The landslide smashed down into the gully bed close to its entrance with a noise like somebody had just blown up the arsenal at Fort Sumter all over again, and dust flew up in a choking cloud as it hit. What was left fell short, rattling down the incline to finish up as a heap of dirt and stones a couple of feet from where we stood. Dust fanned out to cover us like we were caught in a Frisco fog, and I held on to my dun horse as he tugged and snorted at the end of the rein. Seemed like I was choking in a thick blanket that filled my nose and mouth and eyes. It took a minute or so before it cleared, and it was longer than that before I could see to the mouth of the gully. Where that gap had been, that we could have ridden through single file just moments ago, the entrance was blocked solid with a mass of rocks and busted trees that would have reached as high as my hat if I'd still been in the saddle. Swirls of dust lifted upwards, slowly thinning away as we coughed and choked, ears ringing from the echoes of the landslide. I spat out dirt, and peered through watery stinging eyes up for the crest. Same time I did, a spray of dirt kicked up from the ground to my right, and I ducked from habit at the whipcrack lash of the gunshot that came after.

I ran the dun into shelter in the nearest boulder clump, hearing the second shot blast overhead as I went. Ike and Conchita were both down and hunting cover, but that damn fool Armitage still stood in the open, lifting his pistol and scouring the ridge for a target. At that range he wouldn't have stood a chance if he'd been Wild Bill Hickock, and he sure wasn't nothing of the kind. I dived at him, knocking him backwards into the dirt, and I was none too soon at that. Another slug hammered into a boulder behind us, and whined away like a lost soul into the hanging dust.

'Get the horses under cover!' I yelled down at Armitage above the noise of gun-fire. I eased up off him and rolled clear with both hands on my Winchester. 'Into the rocks, Armitage, an' keep 'em there! These bastards kill our horses, we're finished!'

Armitage sprawled away from me, red-faced and covered in dust. From the look on his face he wasn't feeling any too friendly, but I reckoned I could live with that. The shave-tail grabbed the halters of the ponies and ran them into the rocks, taking up the dun's rope once he got there. He'd struggle to hold on to them all, I figured, but that would have to keep. Right now I had other things on my mind.

'Cover me!' I shouted.

I broke from the boulders, heading at a crazy zigzag run for the slope. Flame stabbed at me from a thicket on the rim, and a geyser of dirt flew up a yard or so in front of my face. Crack of the carbine blended with the heavier blast of Buford's Henry rifle, and I saw the bushes shake as whoever it was went diving backwards out of range. A second gunflash licked from a big flat-topped rock on the left, and I heard the bullet go whipping away past my head. I levered and shot in a hurry, and heard the slug hit and ricochet from the rock above. Down in the gully bed Ike and Conchita were into cover and shooting fast, the Henry and the Sharps carbine racketing together as they threw lead up at the rim. I hoisted my Winchester and fired into the bushes, swung and levered to trigger a second shot at the boulder to my left. By now I was back to boiling mad again, and ready for anything. Those two sons of bitches had the gall to bushwhack us, after everything else they'd done! I was busting a gut to get hold of them, and if I did Hargreaves and Cope-stake would be lucky to come out alive, oldsters or not!

I scrambled a few yards further up the slope, loose rocks slithering out beneath my feet as I climbed. Below me Conchita and her man kept up their fire, slugs ripping into the bushes and hammering the boulder with banshee wails. It was a while before any of us noticed that the pair on the ridge had quit shooting back. I pushed to my feet and started to climb for the crest, and the ground slid out from under me, dirt and stones shooting backwards to take me down. I came down the slope in a bumping, slithery fall that didn't do nothing for my bruises, and landed in the gully bed choking in my own private dust bowl. Getting to my feet I swore and spat, beating the dust from my shirt and pants while the last rocks clattered down behind me. It was close to a minute before I got my breath back.

'No way you're gonna make it up there,' Ike Buford told me. He stepped out from cover, mighty slow and careful on his feet, his face still wearing that sick shade of grey. 'No way we'll git the horses to try it, either. They got a half day's start on us, like I said.'

He leaned back on the boulder nearest to him, and sank down on his haunches, his head sinking forward on his chest. Conchita ran and knelt beside him, her arm on his shoulder. That gal's face was troubled, and I reckon she wasn't the only one. We could all see that Buford was close to playing out altogether. And now, with the pass blocked and no way up the slope, we hadn't a chance of catching up with Lydia and the men who'd taken her.

I nodded to Armitage as he came out leading the horses by their ropes, and walked to where Buford sat slumped against the boulder.

'Might as well admit it now, Ike,' I said.

'You were right, and I was wrong. Those sons of bitches have played us for fools, an' it's down to me, I reckon. Anybody wants to kick my butt, they can go right ahead. I'd do it myself if I could reach.'

Ike Buford said nothing, just looked back at me kind of worn out and sick. He was close to the finish, no doubt about it. I glanced at Armitage, figuring he might just take me up on the offer, but the shave-tail frowned and eyed the ridge above, where the last of the gunsmoke drifted away.

'How did those two start that landslide?' the kid wanted to know.

'Easy enough,' I told him. 'They'd shove a log or a tree limb under a boulder on the rim an' lever it out. Once it started rollin', all they'd need to do was sit back an' watch.'

'Or take pot shots at us, I suppose.' Armitage was thinking about Lydia now, and it showed. 'What about Lydia, Miss Soledad? Where was she, while this was happening?'

'Guess they'd have tied her first,' I said. Seeing the heartbreak in his look, I softened my voice a shade. 'Try not to think too hard about it, huh? We'll catch up with her in a while.'

He didn't answer, still wearing that whipped-dog look. Figuring there wasn't much else I could say to him, I turned back to Buford again.

'You know what's comin', Ike,' I said. 'Gonna have to take back them horses, just like you told me.' I paused, watching that stocky, bandaged figure by the rock in front. 'If you reckon you can't make it, me an' Conchita here will have to try it on our own, an' come back later for you an' Armitage.'

'Count me in,' Buford said. He stared back up at me, black eyes hot and fevered in his grey, sweating face. 'No way you leave me behind. I'll make it all right.'

Took me a while to answer him after that, on account of my throat was choked up, and not with dust either. When I spoke, I guess my voice was a little shaky.

'OK, Ike,' I said. I looked the other two over, and shrugged. 'Sorry, folks, but we don't have no choice. We rest up an' let our horses breathe, then we go lookin' for Burgin an' his pals. That's the way it is, I reckon.'

None of them answered. When it came down to it, there was nothing more to be said.

Right now I was feeling more tired than a grizzly in the Fall, and my body felt like it had been hammered to hell, but however it felt I knew it made no difference. Buford had been right first time, and now we had to get back the herd. Those twenty horses were all that stood between the four of us and our coffins, and Lydia would have to wait.

Can't say I looked forward to tangling with Burgin and the rest, but thought of Snake catching up with us was a whole lot worse. Without the horses, there'd be no deal. Lydia's escape had just made things tougher. And by now the Apaches had to be out here and looking.

I beat out the worst of that dust with my hat, and headed for the shade.

'Miss Soledad,' That was Armitage, behind me. 'There's something I must say to you.'

He spoke from over my right shoulder, on account of we were riding double like before, his arms clasped round my waist just about as tight as you might reckon was proper in the circumstances. Figuring it sounded like something worth hearing, I cut a swift glance backwards as we rode. Armitage still looked kind of shaky, his kid's face pale and sick, and that welt had made the mother and father of a bruise that swelled to a lump one side of his head. Still, he was in better shape than he'd been a while back.

'So let's hear it,' I said.

'Miss Soledad.' It sure was an effort for him to spit it out, and from the frown that puckered his face it couldn't have tasted too good. 'It's fair to say that you and I have had our differences on this mission. We haven't always seen eye to eye, I think.'

'Sure, Armitage. That's fair,' I said. I turned back around, scanning the trail that led up through the canyons to where those pine woods beckoned. We'd gone maybe twenty yards further before he spoke again.

'Quite so.' The shave-tail was still struggling, from the sound of it. I could almost hear him flex his muscles for one last try. 'Miss Soledad, I would like you to know that... Well, it seems you were right about most things, and I appear to have been wrong. I mis-judged Burgin and the troopers, and was far too trusting with those other two fellers, Hargreaves and Cope-stake. Thanks to my stupidity, Lydia is in worse danger, and we could all die. I realize this may make no difference now, but I hope you'll allow me to apologize.'

'That's good enough for me, Armitage,' I said.

Fixed as I was, I couldn't help but smile, knowing that poker was out of his butt at last. Maybe he was right and it was too late, but I liked him a whole lot better for it.

'An' don't ride yourself too hard over Lydia, neither,' I told him. 'That's as much my fault as yours. Let's hope we don't both end up sorry.'

We quit talking then, the blackstripe dun stepping through the trail-dust as he carried us forward. Buford and Conchita were out ahead, scanning the rocks and scrub for any sign of movement. The Seminole seemed to have trouble staying aboard his pony, and I saw him grip the saddlehorn once or twice. After the wound he'd taken, I guessed Buford was near the end of his rope, and there was no telling how long he'd be able to last out. Right now Conchita was doing most of the tracking, and she was our best chance of cutting Burgin's trail.

This minute, other things troubled my mind. Like the way the whole business had been figured from the start. Burgin, a bitter veteran due to be turned out to pasture, and the three hard-cases who'd thrown in with him. Four crooked soldiers, and Hood and Griffin to make up the numbers. An oldster and a raw kid, neither one likely to trouble a self-respecting Apache brave. And the shave-tail Armitage for a leader. What chance were we supposed to stand?

Were these the only men that could be used for this mission? Or had there been some reason they were chosen? And if there had, what the hell was it? Hargreaves and Copestake too. Were they just a pair of saddle-tramps, or was there something else I'd missed? And how come they'd known Lydia was Thornhill's daughter?

I scowled and shook my head. Hard as I tried, I wasn't getting any answers. All I knew was, something about this mission stank pretty high, and I aimed to track it down.

We'd begun to climb out of the canyons, moving for the lower reaches of pine, when something shifted in the boulders to the right, and a loose rock came rattling down into the bed of the trail. I twisted sideways, swinging the Winchester over as Armitage fought to hold on. In front, Buford and Conchita turned their ponies to head back.

'Don't shoot, lady!' the voice said.

A dirty, dust-coated figure slithered out from the rocks, and toppled down on to the trail. Couple of seconds later another one followed, the pair of them sprawling in the dust and stones like they couldn't move another step.

'Thank God you found us, lady,' Griffin said. His voice quivered like he was ready to cry. 'We thought we was gonna die out here.'

He drew a long breath and settled himself a little, swallowing. Beside him in the dirt the young kid, Hood, made a sniffling noise and blinked back the tears that filled his eyes and spilled over on to his cheeks. Both had their hands tied behind them with rawhide cords, and their wrists were bloody from where they'd tried to wriggle loose. They were covered with bruises, their clothes ragged from thorn-brush and sharp rocks, and they looked the beatenest fellers I'd ever seen in my life. Must have taken them a hell of a trip to get this far, I thought.

'Get down,' I told Armitage. 'We're cuttin' 'em loose.'

I got down as he loosed his hold and slid from the horse, both of us heading for the men on the ground. Those bonds were so tight I wondered if their circulation had gone altogether, but once my knife sliced the ropes they both sang out loud and clear, and that was good news. They could use both arms, at least.

'Was Treadwell an' Calladine took us out, lieutenant,' Griffin mumbled through cracked, bleeding lips. For now, he seemed not to see the paleness of Armitage's face, and the goose-egg bump on his head. 'Me an' the kid wasn't expectin' nothin' like that, they didn't give us a chance. Once we come round the shootin' was over, an' everybody else was gone.'

'Lucky for us they had trouble catchin' up them hosses.' Hood found his voice at last. Now it was like he couldn't talk enough. 'They was so busy with them critters, must've took 'em a hell of a while to round 'em up – beggin' your pardon, ma'am – an' they didn't pay us no mind. We snuck off into the woods once we could stand, an' since then we been hidin' out an' hopin' we didn't meet no Apaches, nor them soldiers neither.'

'We ain't had food nor water since they tied us up, lieutenant,' Griffin said. He eyed me like a begging dog, licking those dry, cracked lips.

'You got it, soldier,' I said. I unslung my canteen from the saddlehorn and let him drink. Griffin latched on to that water like a sinner to salvation, guzzling it down, and I had to tug it away before it vanished altogether. By now Hood was doing his best to empty Buford's canteen, tears making trails in the dust of his face. It was a while before they finished, but once they did the pair of them looked mighty thankful. Armitage stepped forward and stood over them, hands on his hips. His face was trying for a fair imitation of a floursack, but he held himself together pretty well, I thought.

'Men,' says the shave-tail. 'We're in a tough situation here, no doubt of it. Burgin and his accomplices have the horses, our hostage is in the hands of desperadoes, and Snake and his Apaches are looking for us this very moment. But it's not my way to admit defeat, and by heaven neither is it going to be yours. This is where we start to fight back.'

He paused, letting that sink in slowly, before he went on.

'There are six of us here,' Armitage reminded them. 'Horses enough, ridden double, and enough pistols and carbines for each of us to have a weapon. We're going to get back those horses from Burgin, and once we've done that we're rescuing Miss Mansfield from the renegades. When that's done, Snake can have his horses, and we'll be out of these mountains and back to civilization.' He took another breath, those blue eyes of his real steely as he searched our faces one by one. 'We can do it, and we will too, you hear? Are you with me?'

'You bet, lieutenant!' Hood stared up at him, his eyes awestruck. It was like the kid had just seen Custer and Crook and Nelson Miles all rolled into one. Beside him Griffin nodded and muttered agreement, weariness in his pouchy face. I stayed quiet this time, but I had to admire the feller's sand. Maybe Armitage wasn't always so hot at picking the time for his Custer act, but right now I reckon nobody could have done better. Best of it was, he believed it too. Maybe that was why it worked this time around.

'If it's strategy you're talkin', I got me a plan,' I told him. I waited until Armitage turned around at the end of his speech, and shrugged. 'No tellin' if it's gonna work, but I figure it's the best chance we got.'

The lieutenant thought about it a while, and nodded at last.

'You've been right so far, Miss Soledad,' Armitage said. 'Let's hear what it is you have in mind.'

So I told it, the rest of them listening close, and by the time I finished they were all of then nodding and grinning. Seemed like I'd sold it to them good, all right.

I only hoped it was about to work.

SEVEN

The night-owl hooted as it passed over, flitting like a shadow into the dark. Someplace in the distance a coyote gave a high, yipping cry and his pals set up to answer, the noise coming back in spooky echoes off the canyon walls. Wasn't just the night breeze set me shivering, though the stars shone cold as ice-chips in a black frozen pool of sky. Out here in the mountains, once it gets dark, it ain't so hard to believe in ghosts. I know folks who've seen them, once in a while.

I lay flat beside Conchita in the boulders that fringed the arroyo, my belly bedded on the loose stones. From here we saw the blaze of the fire the soldiers had made, and the huddled shapes around it. Burgin, Calladine and Wild had turned in for the night, lying prone in their bed-rolls in reach of the fire's warmth. Treadwell, the lanky redhead, was sentry, but right now he didn't look too busy. He squatted on his haunches, his back to a boulder maybe twenty yards from his friends, the carbine leaning on the rock as he cupped both hands around a lighted cigarette. Hadn't taken long to find their trail, with Conchita doing the tracking. I figured Burgin would have been in a hurry to quit this country right away, but driving twenty horses ain't no easy job for four men in mountain territory, and once in a while you have to take a rest. And meantime, ain't nothing leaves a plainer trail than a horse herd driven hard.

Those twenty horses weren't far away, either, backed into a dead-end gully that led off to the side of the arroyo. Burgin's men had laid brush to shut off the entrance and keep the herd in place. I studied those critters, watching the firelight slide along muzzles and flanks as they turned and shifted, ready for sleep. My horses, the ones Thornhill had paid me to bring to the Mogollons, and looking just as fine a sight as always. Seemed we'd got to them before the Apaches, anyhow. Let's just hope everything else went the way we'd planned.

Armitage and the rest were further along the dry-wash, dug into the boulders on either side. I'd left the lieutenant my Winchester and young Hood was toting Conchita's Sharps. Griffin was there to hold the horses, they'd stayed behind too. Conchita and me were both carrying our hunting knives and a saddle-blanket apiece, and my .41 pistol was loaded in its holster-pocket. I'd had that gun apart, dried, cleaned and oiled and back together when we made camp after the flash flood. The .41 checked out fine, but I wasn't counting too much on that. As for something to ride, we aimed to catch ourselves fresh horses pretty soon.

The moon rode up over the Mogollon rim, beaming like a white-faced preacher, and I looked across to Conchita. Neither one of us said a word, but she nodded and flashed me that smile, bright and keen as a knife-blade, and we knew this was the time. I slithered from cover, edging forward on elbows and knees and hoping to God I didn't knock any pebbles loose. A few yards off Conchita went ahead smooth and quiet as a snake, seeming to flow over the ground. I didn't try to match her speed, just keeping it as quiet and steady as I could manage. Seemed like no time before we were up with the soldiers and their seven tethered horses, who stood drowsing and shifting from one leg to the other where they'd been tied to the thorn brush by their halters. Looked like

Burgin had a quick getaway in mind, should it be needed, and hadn't hobbled them this time around. I spared a glance for the hulking figure of the sergeant in his bed-roll, and swallowed on my drying throat. This was as close as I aimed to get to Sergeant Burgin, given the choice. Feller was built like a grizzly, and hard as nails into the bargain. Once we'd put a few miles between us, I reckoned I'd be a whole lot happier.

A few yards off, Treadwell hunched over his cigarette, head sinking as he dozed, half-asleep. I edged around nearside of the roan Armitage had left behind, and cut the tether loose. By now the critters were awake, fretting and pricking their ears. Conchita's knife went through the ropes smooth as molasses, hardly making a sound. Between us, we had the seven horses free of their tethers faster than you could shake a stick. I got to my feet, rubbing my hand over the roan horse's flank as I murmured to gentle him down.

'Just take it easy, feller,' I told him. I stowed the knife in its sheath and grabbed his mane, swinging up across his back. Far side, Conchita sprang astride the horse they'd taken from Griffin. Around us other critters neighed and snorted, starting to run loose, and from the nearby corral the herd began to stamp and whinny in answer.

'Let's go!' I shouted.

I drew the .41 Colt pistol and fired it for those frozen stars. Just the one shot, but it went off in the night-time quiet with a noise you wouldn't believe. Gunshot blasted my ears loud enough to empty every boot hill west of the Pecos, and the echoes came thundering back along the arroyo like the end of the world. Pretty soon it wasn't alone. My shot had been the signal for the others to buy in, and they opened up with the echoes the whipcracks of the carbines blending with the heavier smash of Buford's Henry and running together in one deafening drum-roll racket. I saw Treadwell go diving for cover, and Burgin and the others rolled out from their sleeping-places like they'd been shot already. Slugs raised dust and chipped boulders not far away, one bullet ricocheting off the rock nearest Treadwell with a whine that would have shamed the biggest hornet in creation. Conchita and me didn't stick around to watch. We were already waving our blankets and yelling as we drove those horses on for the makeshift corral they had on the herd. The Lipan woman was in there before me, like always, sliding from the horse and letting the blanket fall as she clung to the rein. Conchita dragged out some of the brush, and that was all she had to do. Gunshots were blasting up and down the wash by now, the bed of the arroyo racketing with noise, and the herd came pouring out in a headlong rush, slamming away the brush that was left. I reckon they'd have trampled me flat as a dime, but that gal was greased lightning itself. She was back across the horse in the time it took me to breathe, and then we were both behind the herd and making our blankets fly, driving those beauties past the soldiers and on for the end of the wash.

Burgin reared up out of a cluster of rocks, big as a grizzly and twice as mean, the pistol he held coming up in a hurry. Fresh shots smashed from along the arroyo, and a slug whipped low above his head, close enough to ruffle his hair. He threw himself down in cover and I jumped the roan over him, sweating now in spite of the cold. Seemed my heart was beating my ribs so hard, it was a match for the noise of the shooting all around. Bullets spat and thudded in the dirt ahead, and horses screamed and turned tail, running off to the side. Some of the soldiers' horses got loose, but we kept the herd together, making them run for the end of the wash. I'd figured we were clear when the redhead, Treadwell, lunged up into sight from behind a nearby rock, his thin face hard and pitiless as he brought that carbine into line. He was real close to me, too close to miss, and with no chance to haul my pistol I figured I'd best get ready to die all over again. Then Conchita threw the knife. I heard it whip past me, cutting air with an ugly sound that set my teeth on edge. Treadwell howled and dropped the carbine, tugging at the half-sunk blade as it pinned his shoulder. By the time he pulled it loose and the others broke cover with their guns we were long gone, and the horse herd with us. The whole bunch thundered on for the far end of the wash at a headlong gallop, the dust rolling up in a cloud. Pretty soon I was close to choking and let the blanket drop on my horse's neck, hauling up my bandanna to cover my face.

'That was magnificent, Miss Soledad!' Armitage called. He yelled above the noise of the hooves, dust muffling his voice as he nudged the blackstripe dun out from the boulders, Griffin riding double behind him. Moonlight hit the boyish face, showed that same kid's apple-stealing grin. Seemed like I hadn't seen it in a while, and it was mighty welcome. 'Now perhaps we're getting somewhere.'

I yelled back to him, something about how he should thank Conchita, on account of the fact that I wouldn't have made it without her, but the bandanna muffled my words and the din of the horses' hooves drowned them out. I doubt that Armitage heard any of it. He was already gone, heeling the dun to a gallop as man and horse vanished into the darkness ahead.

By now the others were riding alongside. Hood was aboard Conchita's pony, hanging on tight to the mane like he was scared to fall, and a short way behind was Ike Buford on his own mount. The scout clung to his saddlehorn, and looked anything but steady, and I wondered how much longer he'd be able to hold on. Then again, I had no way of telling if our chances were likely to be any better.

Truth was, we'd managed the easy part, and now we were into the tough end of the business. Sure, we had more horses to ride, and the herd was running in front of us, but now we had the problem of keeping it together. Running a horse herd in the dark ain't easy any time, and was likely to be as much of a trial to the six of us as it had been to Burgin and his pals in daylight. In the maze of gullies that led off from the dry wash, moon and stars weren't too big a help, and the chances of our picking the wrong trail were pretty good. Worse yet, all the troopers' mounts hadn't come along with us, I knew. Two or three had turned back at the shots, running loose. Once Burgin and the others were into the saddle, they'd only themselves to look out for. They'd be holding the aces, and we'd be left with all the grief. Heading around the bend at the far end of the wash, dust sifting through the bandanna to clog my mouth and nostrils, I tried not to think too hard about that.

Didn't take long to work out how right I was. The horse herd stormed down the nearest of the gullies with manes and tails flying like cavalry guidons in a breeze, their dust billowing out to swallow the darkness and our bunch yipping and yelling as they rode along to either side. I was half-blinded and choking for breath when I heard the neighing, snorting uproar in front and drew on the rein, easing the big roan slowly down. Through the hanging dust-cloud I saw my twenty horses turn and mill in a circling bunch, and back of them the looming wall of rock that shut off their escape. Trail we'd taken ended in a box canyon, and now it looked like we were trapped. We'd come down the wrong alley, and no mistake! I tugged the bandanna clear of my mouth, yelling to Conchita.

'Get after 'em, Conchita!' I shouted. 'Keep 'em circlin'! Hood, you go with her! Rest of us'll stand them off!'

Could be Armitage took exception to me giving orders, but I didn't hang around to find out. I was down from the lieutenant's horse and running for cover, leading the animal by its rope. Somewhere to the side movement in the dust-pall told me Griffin and the shave-tail were also hunting shelter. Ike Buford was behind me, sliding down the pony's flank so slow it hurt to watch. The scout forced himself to a lurching run for the boulders just about the same time fresh hooves came drumming in, and Burgin and the others loomed up mighty close at his back, three of them riding and the fourth man stumbling on behind. Any other time, Buford would have outrun them. This time he slipped on a scatter of loose stones, and went floundering down on his hands and knees.

'Goddamn!' The word burst out of him, a winded gasping sound. Ike Buford rolled clear of a shod hoof that threatened to take his head off, snatching at his fallen rifle. He didn't make it, groaning and slumping down as Sergeant Burgin sawed rein to swing the critter back around. I let go the halter on the roan and turned back, running fit to bust as Burgin dragged that horse up on its hind legs, aiming the forehooves at the man on the ground. Wouldn't swear to it, but I reckon the speed I went would have done justice to a quarterhorse in the Kentucky Derby. I was still holding the blanket, and got there in time to swing it across the animal's eyes before those hooves came down. The horse screamed and turned aside, bucking so that Burgin fought to hang on to his seat. Buford rolled weakly away as shots broke out around us, gunblasts echoing up and down the wash. I figured I heard my Winchster among them, and guessed that Armitage was buying in on my account. I saw Burgin drag himself up, trying to line his pistol, and lashed the blanket to smother his hand, shoving his foot out of the nearside stirrup. The big *hombre* swore something fierce, and hit out at me with the hand that held the gun.

Lucky for me the blanket muffled the punch, or he'd have put out my lights for sure. As it was, it felt like a blacksmith's hammer smashed my jaw and sent me down sprawling in the dirt. I scrambled on all fours with my head ringing like the inside of a mission bell, fumbling for the pistol in my pocket and not getting a hold. Reckon I heard Burgin laugh as he lifted that Colt again, and when the hammer clicked it was all I could do to hold on to my butt. Then the Henry rifle blasted and rattled my ears, and man and horse came crashing to earth like an avalanche of boulders falling.

'Got you clean, you sonofabitch!' the Seminole said. He bit the words through his teeth, like it hurt bad to say them. Buford tried to work the Henry for another shot and gave up, gasping as he fell back.

I got my hand on the .41's butt, trying not to move my face and have my jaw drop out. Guns were still racketing, and other shapes loomed through the sifting murk of dust. I saw the thickset figure of Calladine running in with the carbine held crossways in front of him, and the lanky Treadwell not far behind. Wild was still astride his mount maybe a dozen yards off, yelling and whooping as he triggered off shots from his pistol for the boulders. I saw flame stab from that direction, and an invisible steam-hammer punched Wild out of the saddle, the Colt flying from his grasp as he fell. Spiteful crack of my Winchester came after, and I almost smiled. Looked like Armitage had got his eye in, anyhow. Burgin was down and hauling himself clear of the horse that Buford had killed, scrabbling for his own fallen gun. I ran headlong at him, busted jaw and all. Come to think, I must have gone crazy back there. It can happen, I guess.

My boot was travelling for Burgin's head, but the sergeant saw the kick before it was halfway started. He ducked underneath and grabbed my ankle, pulling me clean off my feet. The way I hit the ground, it felt like all my bones were shaken loose, and Burgin wasn't through yet. This time he left the pistol lying, diving on me to shove me flat with one massive hand while the other tugged a long hunting-knife from its sheath. I watched that blade coming my way, and fought like a polecat to get free.

'This is the last grief you give me, you bitch!' Burgin said.

Beyond him, I caught a glimpse of Tread-well from the corner of my eye. The gangling redhead's face was white in the moonlight, his wounded arm hanging useless as he struggled to lift his carbine one-handed. Can't rightly tell whether it was me he had in mind, or Armitage. The way it turned out, it didn't matter. Treadwell barely had the weapon hoisted when there came a hissing thump and he staggered backwards, a feathered arrow suddenly grown out of his chest. The trooper stared down like he couldn't believe it, his mouth wide open but not making a sound. He rocked a half-second on his heels before he went over.

Now the air was choked with the hiss and whisper of flying arrows as I tried to get clear of Burgin and his knife. First lunge sliced my shirt-sleeve as I twisted halfway from him, and I felt the faintest of nicks. Burgin would have gutted me for sure with his next try, but they didn't give him time. I heard that whipping thud as the arrow went home in the middle of his back, and his body jolted against me hard enough to send both of us to the ground. He let go of me, grunting as he forced himself to sit up, the knife fallen as he reached again for the gun. I was already scrambling clear, hooking one hand into Ike Buford's collar to drag him after me as I crawled for cover. Behind me, Sergeant Burgin was busy dying. He died hard, like I figured he would, fumbling with the hammer of the pistol while more arrows went into him. When he keeled over for the last time they'd shot him so full, he looked something between a porcupine and one of my old Aunt Sarah's pin-cushions. Sure wasn't a healthy sight.

I hauled Buford round the far side of that dead horse. It wasn't easy, let me tell you, but being scared stupid helped. Once behind that poor critter, I got down and stayed mighty still, watching the last of the arrows patter and smash in the dirt. Calladine had thrown away his carbine and run to join Armitage in the rocks, and from the look of it the little horse-faced jasper Wild had crawled there already. Conchita and the other two troopers were crouched in the best cover they could find, and the horse herd just milled around and screeched, too scared to make a break up the wash into the bullets and the arrows. But for their noise, it got mighty quiet.

From the boulders on either side along the rim of the dry wash, Apaches eased up into sight. Thin little fellers, mostly, five out of six of them bare-naked but for hide or calico breech-cloths and them high boots they wear, and bandannas round their heads. A few wore store shirts with the colours faded out, and I reckon one had on a Mexican sombrero. What mattered was there was maybe twenty-five of them in all, sporting carbines and bows, and they had us truly hog-tied. If we'd been in trouble before, this had to be plenty worse. Seemed like Snake had got here before us, and stayed watching a while before buying in. And fixed as we were, there was no way we'd get out of the place alive.

From over in the boulders, Armitage looked at me, kind of questioning. His pale, tight-lipped face told me he was trying not to show how scared he felt.

'Yeah, Armitage,' I told him. 'We're in a hole, all right.'

I peered over that dead horse, and waited for what was about to happen next.

EIGHT

I lay flat behind that dead horse, my heart doing its damnedest to bust out of my ribs, and watched those Apaches on the skyline. Seemed like a good half-hour passed before they made a move, though I'm willing to bet it wasn't no more than a couple of minutes. Then one feller shouldered forward from the pack and came down the slope towards us, a couple of others following a mite further back and to either side. I guess with twenty-five against the handful we had, and most of us shot up into the bargain, they didn't have too much to worry about.

'Hold your fire, men!' Armitage sang out. I have to admit, he sounded pretty brave considering. 'They're offering us a truce!'

Way I saw it, there was nothing to show them Apaches were offering any such thing, and with four carbines between us there wasn't too much fire to hold neither, but the shave-tail held his nerve all right. Armitage stood up out of the rocks and into the moonlight, setting my .45-70 down. He lifted his hand in what he figured was the rightful fashion, and started forward to meet them. First sight of it, I almost died of fright myself, but after that the least I could do was back him up. I clambered up from back of the horse, hoping my legs weren't about to give way, and headed over to join him, signing Conchita to follow. Right now, we needed her help more than ever.

The three Apaches came ahead, stepping down into the bed of the wash. Once they were there the feller in front called out, and they all three halted like they'd been turned to stone. Wasn't long before Armitage, Conchita and me were up with them and the six of us just stood looking each other over at a hand's reach. Armitage studied the first Apache real careful, like he might make a mistake here. Feller stared right back with a look that was none too friendly. He was scrawny and small, rigged in a grimy old flannel shirt and hide breech-cloth, and I figured him for older than the rest. There was white in the hair he wore tied back under the calico bandanna, and he stood a little stoop shouldered, but his face was thin and hard as a hatchet and those black eyes probed like a blade, clean through to the bone. Didn't take too much thinking to work out this was Serpiente we were looking at.

'Ask him, is he the one called Snake,' Armitage said. He glanced to Conchita as he spoke, and she broke into Apache. Best I should tell you folks now, I've had dealings with Apache before, and picked up a little of their lingo. But the way Conchita was spitting it out, it got a mite tough to follow.

The old feller eyed the shave-tail like Armitage must have lost his mind, and answered slower. This time I caught the gist all right.

'That is what you call me,' Snake said. His mouth gave kind of a twitch, like he was trying not to smile. 'My name is for me to know.'

He waited while Conchita spelled it out in English for the kid to hear.

'To be sure,' Armitage flushed, the way a kid does when teacher's just put him straight. He shot a sideways glance to Conchita again. 'I am Armitage. We have your horses.'

That thin mouth of Snake's gave a real twist now, and if you heard that Apaches don't smile I'm telling you, don't believe a word of it. I was there, and I saw it plain. Not that it made me easy in my mind.

'That was another time, when we had the woman,' the oldster said. 'Now she is gone there can be no trade. We have you, and we have the horses. What is left for talk, corn-hair?'

Armitage listened as Conchita fed back the words, and I could see his face get whiter and more shocked by the second.

'But this isn't fair!' the lieutenant shouted. 'Damn it, we've kept our part of the bargain!'

At the sound of his raised voice, some of the Indians on the lip of the wash hoisted their carbines and bows ready for a fight, but Snake shook his head and they settled down again.

'She should not have come to these mountains,' the old man said. He looked the shave-tail hard in the eye. 'You, too, should not be here.' After that he seemed to lose interest in the three of us, his glance running over the twenty horses circling at the end of the canyon.

'You have good horses,' Snake decided. He looked away from the herd, and damn if he wasn't studying my blackstripe dun. 'This one is also good. We will take him.' He turned to the *hombre* on his right. 'Tesota, bring him to me.'

'Now just a minute…' I began.

None of them paid me any mind, and the other feller went past me to where the dun stood with his halter dangling to the ground. Tesota was dark and heavy-set, with a solid stocky build, and a busted nose that leaned slantways across his face. Now he got a hold on the dun horse's rope and swung a leg, heaving himself easily into the saddle.

Dangerous or not, I was getting pretty hot under the collar by now, and I'd be damned if I let this go without a fight. Soon as Tesota landed astride the dun, I puckered up and whistled just as hard and shrill as I could bear. It hurt like hell with my jaw the way it was, but it worked like a charm. The big dun wheeled and bucked like a mad thing, whinnying and baring his teeth. Tesota tried his best to stay aboard, but he had no chance. Blackstripe dun pitched the Apache over his neck and into the dirt, rolling and spitting dust as he lost his grip. I whistled again and the dun came to me, gentle as a babe. Up on the ridge, some of the Apaches started laughing.

'He's my horse,' I said. That much Apache I could manage any time. Snake turned around and eyed me mighty close, like he'd just worked out I was there. Seemed like he hadn't figured on me speaking his language.

'They told me Snake's word was good,' I said. Damn, but that jaw hurt like fire every time it moved.

I saw the old feller's eyes narrow down at that, and wondered if I'd have done better to stay quiet. Tesota scrambled up from the dirt, muttering and grabbing for the knife in his belt, but Snake waved him away behind him, watching me all the time.

'You talk big for a woman,' Snake said. He shouted to the warriors on the rim, and the whole band came down, leading their ponies after them. One edged out from the bunch, hauling this wild-looking critter that had neither saddle nor blanket on its back. It was a tall, rawboned paint horse, and it fixed me with the meanest pair of eyes I'd seen. All at once the oldster was smiling again.

'You think you are good with horses,' Snake said. He jerked his chin towards that bucking, fighting pinto on the end of the rope. 'Ride this one. We will watch.'

He looked me up and down, a gleam in his dark eyes like sharpened glass. I studied that vicious-looking critter that plunged against the rope, and wondered if I'd have been better off dying.

'The woman is afraid of him,' Tesota said. He got up real slow, scowling and grimacing as he beat the dust from his breech-cloth. I didn't spare a glance for him, all my attention on that ugly brute of a horse in front.

You bet I'm scared, feller, I thought. All the same, I didn't aim for him to hear me say it. I let the horse be, and took a hold of my dun's halter-rope, calming the critter down. Behind me the rest of our bunch huddled together, waiting for the shooting to start. Ike Buford was down on the ground, shivering and sweating like he was into a fever from his wound. Hood and Griffin were slumped beside him, both of them looking worn out and whipped. Calladine squatted by a rock, white-faced and scared to hell, and Wild was hunched over painfully, one hand to the gash that Armitage's bullet had made across his ribs. Apart from me, Conchita, and the shave-tail, wasn't a single one looked fit to stand. I turned Snake's challenge in my mind, and figured I didn't have much choice.

'I will take your horse, Soledad,' Conchita said. She stepped closer, one hand out to take the rein. I tell you, that gal never turned a hair, standing up straight as a hickory arrow, talking to me and taking the rope like there was nobody else around. Even in this fix, sand like that gave me a warm feeling, and I smiled as I handed the critter over.

'Thanks, Conchita,' I said. 'Stay close, an' keep your ears peeled. Could be I'll need 'em.'

She said nothing, ducking her head in agreement, but there was no need. One look from those eyes of hers was enough; I knew I could count on her. I turned back to the oldster, who'd begun to act a mite impatient.

'The woman who ran from you,' I said. 'The redheaded one, that the white men took. You know where she is?'

Snake lost that twisted grin of his, acting like he didn't hear me. I glanced to Conchita, and she gave it him again. After a while he shrugged and nodded.

'I know the place,' Snake said. 'Later, we would have taken them.'

I eyed that mean sonofabitch pinto, and took a deep breath.

'If I ride the horse, you take us where she is,' I said. This time I made sure it went through Conchita to him; no room for any mistakes.

Snake thought about that, looking from me to the pinto and back again. The old

162

feller nodded his head. I could see he didn't reckon I'd ride that critter, and tell truth, neither did I.

'*Enju*,' Snake answered. 'It is well.'

'I go with you, and Armitage,' I said. Again, Conchita passed the words on to him. 'The ones who stay will not be harmed, and you will let us go alive.'

I waited while he heard Conchita out, flinching at the pain in my jaw. Burgin's knife had nicked the back of my wrist, and I felt the itch of the cut as it dried.

Snake had to think about that, and he didn't look too sure, but in the end he scowled and nodded his grizzled head.

'Afterwards, you go from these mountains and do not come back,' the Apache told me. He found the crooked grin again, his eyes hard and bright on my face. 'It does not matter, woman. You will not ride him.'

'Give me the rope,' I said. This time I didn't leave it to Conchita, looking him hard in the eye.

I moved in to where that vicious critter waited, baring its teeth at me as it dragged on the halter. The Apache that held it struggled with his heels dug in the dirt, and he couldn't wait to hand me that rein just as quick as he knew how. I side-stepped around the pinto as he kicked out, ran at his flank and grabbed mane and rope together, diving up astride. Then I was on his back and riding that horse with everything I'd got.

How did I do it? Maybe you should tell me, feller. Ain't too sure myself, even now. Soon as I landed he bucked so hard it felt like my stomach was left behind and my backbone was shot through my hat. My teeth rattled so fierce they all but shook loose, and the pain in my jaw made me yell out loud. I gripped his barrel tight as a clam with legs and thighs and anything else you care to mention, one hand hooked in his mane and the rope in the other. Sure could have used a pair of stirrups and a good Texas saddle, but I guess bareback was all that was on offer here. That critter twisted and plunged, throwing his head down and kicking up to throw me forward, but I hung in there and he couldn't shake me loose. Most horses I can talk down, given chance, but this feller didn't aim to be reasoned with. He swung his head for a bite at my knee, and I fisted his nose mighty hard to keep him off, feeling every jolt go through me from butt to brain. The pinto bucked and wheeled, trying to slam me against a boulder, but I hauled on the rope and brought us clear. Sweat ran in my eyes and I heard the soldiers and Conchita yelling. Seemed like the Apaches were kind of quiet, but I guess they were still waiting for me to hit the dirt. And right then, so was I.

That horse tried every trick you can name. He dropped on his knees and tried to pitch me over his head. He rolled on the ground and came up again fast as lightning, but I've ridden tricky horses before and saw that one way off. I was clear when he rolled, and back on to him before he made it to his feet. By now it felt like I'd been riding him for a couple of days at least, and my body was jarred to hell and back. Every muscle screamed in my wrists and shoulders, and the spiked pain in my face was enough to make you pass out. From the feel of it, he'd had the skin off both my thighs into the bargain. I gasped and hung tight, hoping he was about to quit. Otherwise, I might just die any time now. Then the steel went out of him and he began to snort and stumble, slowing down. After one heck of a while, he hung his head and stood, his chest heaving as he fought for breath. I looked across to where Snake and his warband stood staring like they'd just seen a ghost, and cracked a painful smile.

'You saw me ride him,' I said. I patted the neck of the pinto, just the once. 'That's a good feller. Just take it easy now.'

I got down from him slow and steady, getting well clear of hooves and teeth before I dropped the rope. After that I kept my eyes on Snake as Conchita fed back most of what he had to say.

'For a woman who talks big, you ride well,' the Apache told me. He indicated the feller on the other side from Tesota, a thin black-haired *hombre* with one good eye. 'When the sun rises, he will take you to where they have the red-haired woman. You will keep your weapons, and the horses you ride, but the twenty horses go with us. This was agreed.'

'That sounds good to me,' I said. Guess I sounded kind of breathless, after the ride I'd had. Snake was still eyeing me mighty thoughtful, like something else had come to mind. Now he looked to the herd grouped at the end of the canyon.

'These are your horses?' I nodded, and the old feller grinned.

'You know horses, woman,' Snake said. 'What do they call you?'

'Soledad.'

'Soledad.' He made a pretty good try at it,

and shrugged. 'You have good horses. When you find the white-eyes and the woman, what happens is your business. But when it is done, you leave these mountains and do not return.'

'I hear you, Snake,' I said.

He said something else I didn't quite catch, and I glanced sideways to Conchita, frowning.

'He says you have Indian hair,' Conchita said. She managed a faint smile as she spoke. 'He asks if you are of the People.'

'Some of me, maybe,' I said.

Snake heard that, and that crooked grin started up again. The Apache nodded, signing to the men around him, and a group moved off to stand guard on the horse herd.

'We will stay here till daylight,' the oldster said. 'Afterwards, we ride different trails.'

He turned from us, rejoining the main group of Apaches, and the bunch of them headed further down the canyon. I breathed out slowly, and found it hurt like hell with the bruises I'd taken. Conchita came over with the dun horse to hand me the rein.

'Thanks, Conchita,' I said. 'Best see to Buford, he looks like he needs it.'

I didn't need to tell her, she was already running to him before I got the words out.

Conchita laid her blanket over the scout as he shivered and sweated, feverish from the old wound. She knelt by him, murmuring to him what I guess were their love-words as I led the dun away. Armitage was first to me, that boyish face of his bright and admiring like he'd just been dazzled by the moonlight.

'Splendid, Miss Soledad! Absolutely splendid!' He stared at me like he'd never seen me before. 'Are you sure you're all right?'

'Reckon I'll live,' I told him. My jaw was coming out in a regular champ of a bruise, and my body felt like I'd been pitched into a threshing machine and out the other side. That pinto had taken the skin off the inside of both thighs, my hands were burned from the rope, and the rest was stiff and sore as a body, could be. All the same, it beat being dead.

'A superb exhibition!' The shave-tail wasn't done. 'I'm lost for words!'

'So don't use 'em.' I headed back to where the rest of the unit was settled, and tied the dun to a bush before sinking down. 'Where we're headed, we'll need all the breath we got.'

'You don't think they'll attack us while we're sleeping?' Armitage eyed the squatting warband uncertainly. I started to laugh and quit once it hurt too much.

'There's twenty-five of 'em, Armitage. If they wanted, they could've rubbed us out a while back.' I sighed, shifting my hammered bones on the hard ground. 'Ain't Snake that's the problem here, mister. Why don't you go ask that pair yonder about the deal they had in Mexico?'

My look went to Calladine and Wild huddled by the rock, Hood and Griffin keeping watch on them with carbines at the ready. Armitage followed that look and frowned. He got up, going over to them.

'This crooked deal you had, to sell the horses to a buyer in Mexico.' The kid's voice bit harder than usual. 'Was it Burgin who planned it, Calladine?'

The burly, white-blond trooper raised his head and looked the lieutenant meanly in the eye. He didn't answer. Alongside him Wild just moaned and fondled the graze on his ribs.

'I asked you a question, soldier!' Armitage was getting impatient. 'You too, Wild. Was this business Burgin's idea? Answer me!'

'Why don't you go to hell, Armitage,' Calladine said.

He eyed the shave-tail levelly, his stubbled

face mean and sulky as before. Armitage stayed looking for a while, and turned away.

'Keep a close guard on these men,' he told Hood and Griffin. 'Once we get back, they'll have charges to answer.'

'If we get back, you mean,' Calladine said.

He turned over and lay down, eyes closing. Armitage left him and came back to join me, settling on the ground and drawing his saddle-blanket over him.

'Best get some sleep, Miss Soledad. We've a hard ride in front of us tomorrow.' He huddled under the blanket, head pillowed on his saddle. 'Good night.'

'Good night, Armitage,' I said.

I glanced to where Conchita hugged the shivering Buford under the blanket, Wild and Calladine with the troopers standing guard, the hunched group of Apaches further off. Last look was for my twenty horses, standing quiet now at the end of the canyon. Sight of their upraised heads and smooth flanks shining silver in the moonlight was the last thing I saw before I closed my eyes, and it left me smiling.

But it was the vicious pinto that I rode all night in my dreams.

The trail brought us around a rocky bend to

someplace high above the world, and we reined our horses, looking out and down. Below the sheer, falling wall of rock the land stretched away in a solid, rolling sweep of green, crowns of the ponderosa pines thrusting up against the sky. Those pine forests marched out to the far distance, green shading to bluish grey as they gave to the broken line of the Sierra Anchas that ridged the skyline. My eyes strained fit to bust to take it all in. If you ain't looked down from the Mogollon Rim, mister, let me tell you that sure is something to see before you die. Just one look was enough to make me catch my breath, and from the way he sat his horse alongside with that steam-hammered expression on his face I reckon Lieutenant Sterling Armitage felt pretty much the same. We'd have stayed there a while longer if the feller Snake sent with us hadn't turned back, tapping the rope-slack against his palm like he hadn't got all day to waste.

Armitage held up a hand to show he got the message, and the Apache nodded, turning to head on along the trail that weaved its way up the wooded flank of the mountain. Feller answered to the nickname of Cuchillo, on account of the knife that

171

had lost him his left eye in some scrape or other. He was thin and undersized like most Apaches I've come up against, and close to you could see he wasn't much more than a kid, maybe eighteen or nineteen years old. The patch that covered the empty socket, and the white scar the blade had made down his cheek put a few years on him at first sight, and gave him kind of a mean look, but he sure as hell knew the country. He'd picked up the tracks the kidnappers and Lydia had left hours ago, and now with the sun starting to wallow down beyond the mountains, I figured we had to be close.

We'd left the canyon at first light, parting company with the others. Ike Buford seemed to have shook off the fever, and while he was still kind of rocky on his legs, he looked to be mending. Seemed only fair to leave Conchita with him after all she'd done to help us, him being her man and all. She'd done her best to tend Wild's graze too, but Armitage made sure him and Calladine were both roped tight before we rode out. Hood and Griffin we left to guard them, and with them and the scouts we figured it should be enough. Right now we didn't have no other choices.

Snake had ridden out just before us, the warband taking my twenty horses with them. Watching them go, I couldn't help but feel kind of sad. Those browns and bays had been close to me for quite a while, and we hadn't been expecting to be parted so soon. Still, that was the way things were, and I guess I had the money, at least. I tried to think about that as the old warchief and his bunch led them off, vanishing into the rocks and scrub fast as you could blink your eye. I knew me and the twenty horses weren't due to meet up again, ever.

Burgin and Treadwell we'd left in the canyon, covered over with a heap of rocks. With the ground so hard, and time running short, wasn't much else we could do.

So now me and Armitage were up on the rim, riding our own horses and packing a pistol and carbine apiece. Any other time I guess the shave-tail would have stayed with the unit, but right now the lives of the whole bunch hung on our finding Lydia and getting her back, and Armitage and me were just about the only two left to do the job. And I got the feeling the lieutenant might just have a personal interest.

Reckon my mind must have drifted, and I'd started to think about the ranch and

Ramon, and that little buckskin colt of mine. That was before the shave-tail's voice brought me back again.

'Let's hope we find her soon,' Armitage muttered, his face mighty grim. 'The thought of what she might be suffering! I find it hard to bear, Miss Soledad.'

'Those fellers you mention are after the money, Armitage,' I reminded him. 'Way I see it, they ain't gonna hurt her none.'

'You don't think?' His voice seemed to tighten up and choke.

'No, I don't. I doubt they had the time, an' I ain't too sure they're up to it, neither.' I risked a slow, painful grin. By now I figured my jaw wasn't broken, and all it could do was hurt. 'Relax, soldier. Lydia come out smiling the last time, an' that was from the Apaches, remember? She'll be all right, count on it.'

'I'm grateful to you, Miss Soledad.' Armitage smiled kind of shaky, brushing a hand at the sweat on his brow. 'Heaven knows, you've saved our lives more than once already.' He paused, seeming to collect his thoughts a little before he went on. 'I daresay by now you will be aware of my feelings for Miss Mansfield?'

'Daresay I do.'

'I had hoped…' Armitage broke off, and tried again. 'At one time it seemed my feelings might be returned. But something happened, I'm not sure what it was exactly, and things cooled between us. This was shortly before she left the fort, you understand? Before the Apaches caught her.'

I didn't say a word, watching Cuchillo's thin back as he rode ahead, but you can bet I was thinking plenty.

'This has been a bad business altogether!' The lieutenant burst out at last. His voice still sounded puzzled. 'I can't comprehend why Burgin behaved as he did. What on earth possessed the man?'

'That's easy,' I said. 'Money, and plenty of it. Down in Mexico you'd get big money for those horses, more than Burgin an' his pals could make in a lifetime. Seems like he figured it was worth killin' for. Then again, I ain't too sure he was the big wheel behind it.'

'Miss Soledad! Whatever do you mean?' Armitage stared at me, shocked out of his worries for the moment.

'Think it over,' I told him. 'Sure, Burgin was hard enough to keep the rest in line, but plannin' somethin' like that takes brains to do it. How come Calladine wouldn't talk, even when Burgin was dead? Maybe this mission of ours ain't meant to work at all, Armitage.'

'But that would mean Lydia would have died!' Armitage shouted. His voice was so loud that Cuchillo turned around, and the shave-tail went quiet.

'Ain't sure about this,' I told him. 'But I reckon Lydia might give us some answers. Maybe she didn't come here by choice, Armitage. Maybe she was runnin' from somethin'. An' if so, she's the only one who'll tell us why.'

We were around the next bend in the trail, heading into the trees, when Cuchillo raised his hand and brought his mount to a halt. We edged up to join him.

'They are here,' the Apache said. He pointed further ahead through the wooded stretch. 'Into the trees, not far. Two white men, and the woman.'

He turned his pony around, man and horse easing past us as he started back down the trail. When he was almost by, Cuchillo reined in and looked me in the face with his one good eye.

'Snake says, there is one who follows,' he told me. 'Look out for him.'

He touched heels to his mount, heading

back down the trail. Pretty soon he was round the bend and out of sight.

'Now it's you an' me, Armitage,' I said.

I got down from the dun, flinching a mite at the chafing of my thighs, and slid the carbine from its scabbard. Armitage drew his pistol, and stepped down to join me. We left the trail and went into the trees, each leading our horse behind. Wasn't long before a cleared stretch showed up ahead, where a tumbledown shack seemed to wedge itself against a single huge boulder. Out front I saw the two tethered horses, and knew we'd found them. Thankfully there was no breeze blowing, so we had that much luck at least. I tied the dun to the nearest pine-trunk and Armitage followed suit. Then we set out towards the shack with our guns at the ready.

We were halfway there when the door came open and Hargreaves stepped out, slapping the hat on his shiny dome. Lydia followed, with Copestake right behind, glowering through his whiskers. They hadn't changed a bit since we'd seen them last. That redhead gal was just as pretty as always, and they were just as unappetizing, Hargreaves and his wrinkled turtle face and his pal with enough brush on his chops to put the Big Thicket to shame. Copestake and Lydia stayed by the door, but it looked like Hargreaves was about to leave. The stretched-out, gummy son of a bitch was grinning as he walked to where his horse was tied, and laid a hand on the rope.

'Don't you worry none, little lady,' the gaunt feller was saying. 'In a few more days I'll get word to your daddy, and he'll find the money. Then I reckon you kin go on home. If the 'paches don't catch up with you agin, that is!'

Lydia Mansfield didn't say a word, but those green eyes of hers looked the pair of them over so fierce she didn't have no need. If you could kill with a look, I reckon Hargreaves and Copestake would both have been mighty short of breath right then and there. As it was, they didn't get too much time to worry about it. Hargreaves had barely touched the rope when the two horses began fretting and tossing their heads, ears pricked as they caught our scent. Sometimes horses are a way quicker than folks, take it from me.

'Stand away from her, both of you!' Armitage ordered. He took a step forward, his mouth drawn tight and his blue eyes cold as a January lake as he aimed the pistol at Hargreaves' belly. 'And throw down your guns!'

The gaunt-faced *hombre* spun round like he was already hit, staring bug-eyed to where we'd just appeared. What he saw was black gun-muzzles, and I guess our faces back of them were none too friendly. Hargreaves gulped and fingertipped his pistol loose, kicking it away as it dropped to the ground. Vern Copestake scowled real mean, and his hand quivered towards the gun in his belt. Sight of my Winchester lined on his middle was enough to change his mind.

'You heard him, Copestake,' I said. 'Leave that pistol be, or there's gonna be a breeze blowin' clear through you to that cabin wall! Shuck off the belt, an' let it drop!'

Copestake looked at me and smouldered a little, like he might just set his whiskers alight. Then he unlatched the belt, and belt and gun hit the dirt together. Lydia turned our way, and I reckon I'll never see a look of joy like that on any gal's face unless I bust into her boudoir unexpected. Wasn't me had her attention, though. That look was all for Armitage.

'Sterling!' Hadn't heard her talk that way before, kind of swoony and breathless all in one. Lydia clasped her hands, green eyes wide like she was about to faint. 'Oh Sterling, you came back. Thank God you're here!'

'Stand away from her, you blackguard!' Armitage acted like he hadn't heard a thing, voice biting like a woodman's axe. Back of the pistol he stood straight and tall, and you could tell he was a soldier now. I had to admit, he looked pretty handsome too. 'Back to the wall, Hargreaves, and join your friend. Believe me, it would give me great pleasure to shoot both of you down!'

'Now take it easy, mister.' Moses Hargreaves went stumbling backwards, almost falling as his back hit the wall. The oldster puckered his turtle face, both hands raised as he tried to smile and didn't make it. 'We wasn't about to do her no harm.'

'I know what you intended,' Armitage told him. 'If it's left to me, you'll live to regret it. Now don't move, and keep quiet!' He beckoned to Lydia, voice softening just a touch. 'Come away from them, Lydia. You're safe now.'

I had to allow he was handling it pretty well, and was set to stay watching, when those tethered horses started acting restless again, and I pricked my ears along with them. Back into the trees, so faint I barely caught it, another horse snorted and stamped its hoof.

'Reckon we got company,' I told Armitage. I lowered the Winchester and turned around, making for the woods. 'Keep an eye on these buzzards, Armitage. I best go take a look.'

'Don't worry about that, Miss Soledad.' The blond kid eyed the kidnappers coldly as Lydia edged over to join him. 'I don't intend to let either of them out of my sight.'

'Good enough,' I said.

I headed back into the woods, picking my way through the trees and brush for where I reckoned that noise had come. Trail led deeper into the woods out to the left, but I guess it wasn't so far. Couldn't have been more than five minutes before I caught sight of a deadfall that made a cleared stretch in the trees, and a lone horse standing tethered real tight to a ponderosa pine. That horse was a critter I'd have known anywhere. Tall chestnut stallion with a blaze on the forehead, and the way he was tied only made me surer. I'd seen that stallion the once, when he came in through the gate of the ranch a few days ago. And now it all came back to me, what Cuchillo had said about one who followed, and how we had to look out for him.

I was still thinking that over when something shifted in the brush on my right, and gun-hammer clicked real loud in the quiet.

'Drop the carbine, Miss Soledad,' Colonel Harlan Thornhill said. 'I'd hate having to shoot you in self-defence.'

I took one look at those steely eyes, and let the carbine hit the leaves. Thornhill smiled like a killer cat and kicked it behind him, stepping out on to the trail.

'Now let's rejoin the others, shall we?' He waved the gun barrel back the way I'd come, nodding for me to move. 'I daresay they'll be expecting us.'

I went where he told me, feeling sicker than I'd done at any time since we crossed the Verde. It had been for nothing, everything we'd done a waste of time. Thornhill had outsmarted us, and now he had it all.

I was back in the hole, and no mistake. Maybe this time there'd be no way out.

NINE

Thornhill had it right. Armitage and the others were expecting me back. All the same, when I walked out from the trees with both hands lifted and Thornhill out of reach behind me with his gun on my back, they all seemed mighty surprised.

'Drop the gun, lieutenant,' Thornhill said. There wasn't a pinch of humour in his face. 'Otherwise I'll have to shoot Miss Soledad, and don't think I wouldn't.'

Armitage stared for a couple of seconds, looking kind of stunned. Then his face went hard and he gripped the pistol a little tighter. Beside him, Lydia didn't so much as breathe, white-faced and scared with her hand to her mouth like she'd seen the worst kind of ghost.

'Do as I say, Armitage!' The colonel's voice cracked, running short on patience. 'Or maybe you'd like to see her die?'

'He means it, Armitage,' I said.

Armitage glanced my way then, and I have to tell you there ain't many times in my life

I've felt so useless. The shave-tail breathed out short and fierce, and threw the gun away from him to the ground.

'Much better, Armitage.' Thornhill flipped the pistol barrel, motioning me forward. 'Now you and Lydia stay there, and Miss Soledad can join you.'

I walked over to where the other two stood waiting. Every step, I was hoping the ground would open up and swallow me whole. Over by the cabin wall the two oldsters stood watching Thornhill warily, like they were none too sure.

'Sure glad you showed up, Thornhill,' Hargreaves offered. He tried again for a smile, and still couldn't make it. You ever seen a turtle smile, feller? No, neither have I. Thornhill looked the pair of them over, kind of cold.

'Pick up your weapons, gentlemen,' the colonel said. His eyes were sharp as a winter frost. 'Your attempt to blackmail me appears to have failed miserably, but it seems we're in partnership again. Only this time I give the orders. Is that understood?'

'You got it, Thornhill,' Hargreaves nodded in a hurry. Copestake stayed quiet like always, just nodding along with him, but you could tell the pair of them were mighty

184

relieved not to be wrong side of the gun. The gangling oldster scrambled to pick up his pistol from the dirt, grinning toothlessly as he got to his feet and his whiskery pal did likewise. Pretty soon we had three unfriendly guns pointed in our direction.

'I hoped I'd seen the last of you, Harlan,' Lydia said. Her face was ash-white, and the sick expression there told me for sure she had some of the answers. Not that it was a deal of use right now. Thornhill didn't turn a hair, just smiled like a lobo wolf and shook his head.

'I'm afraid not, my dear.' Thornhill shifted his cold eyes to Armitage and me. 'I imagine by now you will have worked this out for yourselves?'

'Why don't you tell it, Thornhill?' I said.

'If you insist,' the colonel shrugged. Back of the gun he was tall and handsome as he'd ever been, but now what I saw was beauty of another kind. The way a puma looks, or a wolf stalking a broken-legged deer. 'As commander at Fort Garland, I had oversight of army contracts to the reservation Indians. It wasn't too difficult to divert a number of beef deliveries elsewhere and report them stolen, with a little help.' He paused, nodding to the grinning pair beyond him.

'These two proved useful to me; they posed as ranchers, and between us we had the beef shipped to Old Mexico and sold at a very lucrative price.'

'Sure,' I nodded, catching on too late again. 'Old Mexico, that's where Burgin was headed with my horses, ain't it?'

'It's where we did most of our business.' Thornhill ducked his head, like he was mocking a smart little kid. 'Snake and his friends were on the reservation at the time, of course. They protested often enough, but there was no proof pointing to me. Besides, who would believe the word of a bunch of savages against an officer with years of service? No, there were no problems on that score.'

'Somethin' went wrong though, didn't it?' I said. I looked to Lydia as I spoke, and the redhead shuddered, closing her eyes. She was all set to tell me when Thornhill cut in again.

'A man called Hagan, he was quartermaster at the fort.' Thornhill had quit smiling, his voice colder yet. 'He'd been useful to me, helped falsify the accounts on occasion, but after a while he held out for a larger measure of the proceeds and threatened to expose me if he wasn't paid.' He raked me over with those pale, steely eyes. 'As you can imagine, this made matters rather difficult. I couldn't permit it.'

'He killed him!' Lydia burst out with it suddenly, her voice gone loud and scared. She met Thornhill with that same scared look I'd seen already, all but sobbing the words. 'In the stables at Fort Garland, he speared him with a hayfork and claimed it was an accident. But I saw it – he murdered him. It was horrible!'

Thornhill said nothing, just studied her with those pitiless eyes.

'I was grooming my horse when they came in.' Seemed like Lydia couldn't get the words out quick enough. 'It was dark in there. Neither of them saw me, I stayed hidden all the time. I heard them arguing, and Hagan demanding money then he stuck the fork into Hagan's belly. Blood was everywhere, and his screams – I can still hear them now! It was only afterwards Harlan found out I'd been there, but once he did I knew I had to get away. If I hadn't, he'd have killed me too!'

'So that's why you ran,' I said.

'Precisely.' Thornhill cut in again, his voice impatient. 'I had hoped to collect my – earnings, shall we call them – and take an unscheduled retirement south of the border, but for that I needed time. Lydia was the one fly in the ointment. As long as she was still alive, my claim that Hagan's death was an accident could always have been challenged. So, when the Apaches sent their ransom demand, I saw my chance.'

'Yeah, that much I figured.' I faced those three guns as I spoke, and it didn't make me feel any too comfortable. 'You aimed for the rescue mission to fail right from the start. Burgin an' his pals were gonna rub us out, sell the horses across the border an' disappear with them. Then Snake kills Lydia, an' all your troubles are over, huh?'

'Right again, Miss Soledad.' He gave a mocking bob of the head, but the pistol he held didn't move an inch. 'It wasn't too hard to find the men I needed. Burgin was an easy mark; close to retirement from the service, a drinker, always short of ready money. What I offered was better than he'd ever have got from the army. The others were troublemakers, due for the stockade or worse, and were ready to go along. Unfortunately, they were not equal to the task.'

I heard him out, meeting those eyes the best I could. For one thing, I figured it was better to listen than stop a bullet. I had another reason, too. Thornhill had taken the carbine, but my .41 Colt pistol was still nestling in the pocket holster on my right hip. None of them had seen me use it, and I reckon they'd missed it. I sure hoped so, because it was the only chance we were likely to get. And for that, I needed to keep the feller talking.

'Why'd you come out here?' I wanted to know.

'Simple enough.' Thornhill had lost the smile, his tanned face darkening in annoyance. 'People had begun to ask awkward questions about Hagan, and Lydia's disappearance. By the time I'd gathered my funds together, I was being pressed for answers. I felt it advisable to be elsewhere for a time. And once I found your camp beyond the Verde and discovered that Burgin had failed, I decided to follow you myself.' He paused, that steely stare moving from me to Armitage and back again. 'You two have caused me a great deal of trouble. Time we put a stop to it, don't you think?'

I might have said something back to him, but sight of that pistol dried up my throat like a buffalo wallow in August, and I couldn't so much as croak. Then again, while Thornhill sure had most of my attention, he didn't have it all. Over by the hitching-post those horses were acting mighty skittish, tugging and blowing through their nostrils as their ears pricked up. Something was happening, all right. No way of telling what it was, but it surely couldn't make things much worse.

'You got my vote there, Thornhill.' Mose Hargreaves cackled, baring toothless gums. He dug into the pocket of his threadbare Levis, bringing out that filthy spotted bandanna and what it held. The old goat stuck the pistol in his belt a moment, shaking out the false teeth into his palm.

'Kind of a special occasion, ain't it? Least I kin do is fix myself a regular smile, I reckon.'

He grinned, fumbling with both hands to fit the dentures into place. Wasn't the prettiest of sights, better believe it. Copestake just scowled and fidgeted, and Thornhill had quit smiling too. Now he'd got his own speech over, I guess he was anxious to finish the job. He stood back and took aim at me, bringing up the pistol.

'Goodbye, Miss Soledad,' Thornhill said.

One of the horses neighed shrilly, kicking as it fought to pull loose. Right after that, quicker than you could snap your fingers, something cut air between Thornhill and me, and Hargreaves's old hat went bounding from his head and rolled in the dirt. A cracking noise came after, like somebody had just snapped a stick clean across, and I knew it had to be a carbine. Thornhill swung, blazing blind into the trees, and we got our chance. I threw myself down and tugged that .41 pistol free just as fast as I could grab the butt. I got a bead on the colonel before he could turn, and squeezed off a shot. Hump in the ground jarred my elbow, and it didn't hit where I wanted, but it was good enough. Thornhill clutched his leg and yelled, going over. His gun went off as he fell, the shot blasting dirt. By then I was rolling clear with the .41 filling my hand as all hell broke loose around me.

Hargreaves dropped his false teeth when the first shot sounded. Now the oldster scrabbled after them in the dirt, mumbling something I couldn't hear as he clawed to catch hold. Lydia kicked them away and Hargreaves heaved up on his knees, looking hurt and angry all in one as he fumbled for the gun in his belt. Guess he wasn't thinking too straight. When he moved, he blocked off Copestake from clear sight of the other two, and Armitage came diving in to snatch his own pistol from the ground. The lieutenant shoved Lydia behind him, fixing on being brave or crazy or maybe both at once. He had the gun lined on Copestake as the whiskered *hombre* got around his friend, and the pair of them fired together. Noise of the gunblasts battered across the clearing, so loud I could feel my ears rattle. Armitage pitched away to the ground and I heard Lydia scream. I knew then I hadn't been deafened, at least. Vern Copestake staggered back against the cabin wall, his whiskery face twisted in pain as he clutched a bunch of bloody shirt front where the slug had hit. He was still fighting to lift his own gun for another try when that carbine whiplashed out again. The slug took off the top of Copestake's head and splattered it in a god-awful mess across the outside of the cabin wall. What was left of him dropped like a sack, and seemed like you couldn't see for blood. Might just have turned me sick to my stomach if I'd had time to think it over.

Hargreaves had the pistol from his belt, and was aiming for Lydia, who knelt like a hypnotized rabbit in front of him. Armitage was struggling up, blood running down his face from a gash in the cheek, but there was no way he'd be fast enough. I brought my own Colt into line, aiming for the oldster's middle, and yelled to him through the wafting smoke-cloud.

'No!' I shouted, choking in yellow gun-smoke. 'Drop it, Hargreaves, you hear?'

He looked my way, and saw the pistol levelled on him. From here I could see the sweat on his bald, shiny dome, and that turtle face clenched up in rage. He heard me all right, but he didn't do like I told him. Maybe he figured I didn't know how to use that .41. Or maybe he was just had enough to kill, no matter what. Either way, he swore and swung, aiming at Lydia Mansfield. And I swore too, pressing the trigger. Something took hold of Mose Hargreaves and threw him backwards like he'd just been hit by a locomotive, the pistol flying out of his hand. Noise of my own gunshot blasted back at me, and I shivered, the hairs up on my neck. Hargreaves hauled himself on all fours, blood spilling from his toothless mouth, and got a hold on the gun. I watched him lift the weapon again, thumb slipping on the hammer as his grimy shirt grew an ugly stain across the front. I tried to call to him again, but my throat wouldn't work and nothing came out. Besides, I knew he wouldn't pay no mind. I triggered again as he fought to work the hammer, and the slug doubled him over, his lanky frame folding itself forward. God help me, I shot that old feller one more time, and Hargreaves keeled over slowly, going down to meet the dirt face-first. He shuddered once as he landed, and was still.

Thornhill heaved up from the ground, limping on one leg as he looked for Armitage. The kid had him beat for speed, but his aim was none too good. Maybe it was the blood in his eyes, but his first shot wailed over the colonel's shoulder, and Thornhill was shooting before he got another chance. Armitage grabbed at his arm and went over again, the pistol flying from his hand. Lydia gave out a wild yell and slithered after it, but Thornhill wasn't too interested in her right now. Instead he swung awkwardly round and lined on me, just as I thumbed hammer and heard that goddamned click that told I'd hit on an empty. I saw that mean smile, the cold eyes above the pistol aimed at my head, and got ready for the finish. Then I heard that carbine crack again.

Colonel Harlan Thornhill screamed like a coyote in a gin-trap. He turned, clutching a smashed elbow that dripped blood on to the ground, and stumbled away. He fought to hold on to the gun as he went, but I reckon the pain was too much, and he let it drop before he was halfway across the clearing. Another slug cut leaves from the brush beyond him, crack of the carbine coming after. Lydia tried a shot too, that dug dirt up by his feet. Then Thornhill was clear, and staggering like a drunk into the trees. Sitting in the dirt, shucking the dead shells from my Colt, I was so pleased to be breathing that right then he could have gone to hell for all I cared.

I turned my head and saw Conchita come out from the trees further back, running like a deer and leading the pony by its rope. The Sharps carbine was in her right hand, still trailing smoke. When she got to me she halted and looked down, a question in her eyes, and I nodded back.

'Sure, Conchita, I'll live,' I said. 'Thanks a lot.'

She glanced into the trees, the way Thornhill had gone. 'Let him go,' Conchita said. There wasn't any pity in her voice. 'There is nowhere for him to hide.'

Lydia had dropped the pistol, scrambling over to where Armitage struggled to get up from the ground. She hugged him close, tears running down that lovely face as she called his name and brushed at his long blond hair.

'Sterling!' The redhead sobbed like her heart would break. 'Oh, Sterling honey! What did he do to you? Tell me he didn't hurt you bad.'

She hugged him so tight I thought she might choke the breath out of him, and Armitage moaned and tried to sit up. From here I could see one slug that gashed his face, and Thornhill's second try had cut a furrow in the back of his hand, but neither wound looked too serious. Armitage would live, I guessed, if Lydia didn't smother him first.

'The grey one passed the canyon on his way north,' Conchita said. She lowered the carbine, holding the pony on a long rein as she studied the sprawl of bodies in the open. 'I found his tracks, and knew he meant to kill you, so I left the others and followed.'

'I was never so glad to see you, an' that's the truth,' I said. I got up slowly, feeling kind of dizzy as I reloaded my Colt with fresh bullets and looked around. 'How 'bout Buford an' the rest?'

'They wait at the canyon.' Conchita said. For the first time that faint, unsure smile lit her face. 'Buford is well. We will go from these mountains together.'

I nodded, finding it hard to answer, sick as I was from the stink of blood and gunsmoke. You ever smelled spilled blood and gunsmoke together mister? Take my advice, it's best you don't try it. Sure ain't pleasant, especially when you just done some of the spilling yourself. I walked on shaky legs to where Hargreaves lay, and turned him over. That oldster was mighty dead, but his eyes stared up at me like he couldn't figure out what I'd been thinking of, gunning him down that way. I looked into his eyes and didn't know whether to throw up or cry. Hargreaves shouldn't have been out here getting himself killed. The old fool should have been in his rocker, smoking a pipe and watching the sun go down on his front porch someplace. Hadn't never been a time I'd killed a feller that old, and I have to admit it shook me up pretty hard for a while.

No need for me to look at Copestake. That mess of blood on the wall, and what was left of him, told all the story I needed to know.

By now Armitage was sitting up and trying to push Lydia off, but it didn't look like he was trying too hard. Conchita tethered her pony and we both followed Thornhill's tracks into the woods. Chestnut horse was still tied, and we saw the blood-smears where the colonel had tried to work the tether loose and failed. Like always, the critter was tied too tight. Horse made no fuss when we untethered him, I reckon he was glad to breathe easy for once. Inside the saddlebags I found wads of thick, crisp tens and twenties packed against the leather. Thornhill had brought along something for a rainy day, all right. Him we didn't find. His bloody trail went deeper into the woods, out of sight, and we let him go. The colonel was out of the game. Way I saw it, he had a whole lot more worries than we did.

We rested up a while as best we could, and Lydia cleaned up Armitage's cuts. Tell truth, she wouldn't let either of us near him. The bodies we covered over with rocks and dirt. I felt mighty glad when we mounted up and left that clearing behind, leading the two spare horses. Reckon I couldn't wait to get out of these mountains.

Late into the night, we heard the screaming. It roused us all awake, and set the horses to snorting and stamping and pulling on their ropes. Armitage was standing guard, holding his pistol left-handed with the other bound up in his bandanna. When I glanced across to him I saw him shiver, and wipe at his face with the back of his unwounded hand.

'Over that way,' Armitage said. His face shone silver-white and ghostly, and I reckon it wasn't just down to the moonlight.

I followed his pointing finger to a spot lower in the timber, where a faint orange glow showed through the trees. Just as I looked, those screams came bursting out again. This time I shivered too.

'Reckon he ran into Snake an' his bunch,' I said. Now I felt sick, all right. Conchita and Lydia moved in to stand beside us, the Apache woman toting the carbine just in case. Lydia gripped my arm so hard it felt like her fingers dug into the bone. She stared and listened to those awful screechings going on and on.

'He was good to me, sometimes,' Lydia said. Her voice shook, and I saw her eyes fill up, glistening in the moonlight. 'He raised me from a child, after my father died.' Screams broke out again, worse than before, and she shivered, looking my way like she was begging me to stop it. 'Soledad, I know what he did was bad. I know he'd have killed us all. But to die like this...'

She quit halfway through, and began to sob, both hands covering her face. I got a hold of her and hugged her, trying to calm her down the way I'd quieten one of my horses. Guess there wasn't much else I could have done, right then.

'Just take it easy, girl,' I told her as her tears soaked the front of my shirt. 'Ain't nothin' we kin do for him now, an' pretty soon we'll be out of these mountains. Now you go lie down an' try to get some sleep, you hear?' I turned to Armitage, who still stood white-faced holding the pistol. 'Go with her, Armitage. Me an' Conchita will take over here.'

Armitage took Lydia by the arm and led her back, settling down a decent distance from her as she huddled under her blanket. Noise of those screams went on, tearing at the night, and I felt my mouth go dry as a gypsum dune in summertime. It was a while before they quit, a couple of hours or more, and even after that it seemed like I could hear them.

We none of us got much in the way of sleep that night.

TEN

We found Thornhill early the next morning. We hadn't ridden more than a couple of miles when our horses shied and pulled against the reins, their nostrils and ours filling with an ugly burned-out stink. Something lay one side of the trail, overhung by a black buzzing cloud of flies, and as we came closer we saw that Colonel Harlan Thornhill wouldn't trouble anyone ever again. The Apaches had pegged him over a fire-pit and roasted him slow, and you can take it from me he wasn't handsome no more. I'd just as soon not mention how he looked, but there ain't no way I'll forget it. Times, at night, it comes back to me again. Lydia cried some more, her having known him best, and me and Armitage tried our best not to throw up our breakfasts. He almost made it, too.

Conchita didn't say a word. When she turned her head my way, and saw me all flour-faced and swallowing hard, that look in her eyes said 'what did I tell you?'

Wasn't time for nothing fancy. We covered

what was left of him with brush and rocks, and headed out of there just as soon as we could.

Buford and the others met us back at the canyon. Ike was looking mighty spry, if a mite sore from that scratch he'd taken, and Hood and Griffin were both in pretty good shape. Couldn't rightly say the same for Wild and Calladine, but they'd had the starch taken out of them by now. After what those two had seen, I guess the stockade didn't seem so bad. We had no trouble from them all the way home. Come to think, we had no trouble from Snake either. None of us set eyes on a single Apache all the time we were riding, but I'm willing to bet they watched us every step out of those mountains.

As for Armitage, he was a little shot up but not so bad he wouldn't mend. Lydia had fixed up the cut hand real good, and patched the gash in his cheek. He'd have a pretty good scar in a while, I figured, and it wouldn't surprise me if he didn't go showing it off to the other shave-tails, the way they reckon them German fellers do. And Lydia, well, she was real close to him all the time after that, like she couldn't get enough of him, and if you ask me he didn't mind a bit. From the way the pair of them carried on I reckoned shoes and rice could be in order once they made it to the nearest mission. And why the hell not? Armitage wasn't so bad once he'd worked that poker loose, and even a gal like Lydia could do a sight worse for herself.

Pretty soon we crossed the Verde, out of the Mogollons, and I said my goodbyes to Ike and Conchita. Buford just grinned and shook hands, but Conchita caught hold and hugged my neck so tight I was short on breath for a while. When she let go she had the broadest smile you're ever like to see.

'You *are* of The People, Soledad,' Conchita said. 'I know it.'

'If you say so, Conchita,' I told her. After everything she'd done for me, I was damned if I was going to argue about it.

The others I left at the nearest settlement, Armitage and the troopers taking charge of Thornhill's chestnut and the saddle-bags with the stolen money. Armitage shook left-handed, his right still being kind of painful, and managed a smile; but damn if Lydia didn't reach out and hug me close, just the same.

'Thanks for everything, Soledad,' the redhead told me. 'It's good to know that we're friends.'

'Sure is, Lydia.' I grinned and shrugged, getting free, and looked the two of them over. 'Just be sure to take good care of him, now.'

Armitage grinned too, and coloured up kind of embarrassed, and Lydia smiled, covering his good hand with hers.

'Don't worry, Soledad,' Lydia said. 'Once we get back to Fort Garland I don't aim to let him out of my sight.'

So that was okay too. Hear tell they're due to marry anytime now.

Once I got back to the ranch I found that buckskin colt was up and running, and everything else there was just fine. And since then, I'd have to admit that things have been pretty peaceful around here. Quiet, almost, you might say. Army ain't come calling for the money, not that I aim to give it back. A deal's a deal, I reckon.

Then again, that feller trouble is always on the prowl, and it seems to me he ain't given up on me yet. Times, I get to wondering if I'll ever shake that old bastard off my trail.

Reckon not.

This Large Print Book for the partially sighted, who cannot read normal print, is published under the auspices of

THE ULVERSCROFT FOUNDATION